Another Chance

Ahmed Faiyaz grew up in Bangalore and now lives in Dubai. He's a strategist by profession, with a number of years in management consulting behind him. He is the bestselling author of *Love, Life and All That Jazz* and *Scammed*. His stories are also featured in the bestselling Urban Shots series.

Another Chance

AHMED FAIYAZ

RUPA

Published by
Rupa Publications India Pvt. Ltd 2014
7/16, Ansari Road, Daryaganj
New Delhi 110002

Sales Centres:

Allahabad Bengaluru Chennai
Hyderabad Jaipur Kathmandu
Kolkata Mumbai

First published by Grey Oak Publishers India Pvt. Ltd in 2011

This is a work of fiction. Names, characters, places and incidents are either the
product of the author's imagination or are used fictitiously,
and any resemblance to any actual persons, living or dead,
events or locales is entirely coincidental.

ISBN: 978-81-291-3535-3

First impression 2014

10 9 8 7 6 5 4 3 2 1

The moral right of the author has been asserted.

DEDICATED TO

My wife—Minaz Nawab Faiyaz; we've been miles apart in more ways than one, while I wrote this book. I thank her for her love and understanding in supporting my madness, and enduring everything with a smile through this journey. Without her support I wouldn't be able to isolate myself and do exactly what I want to do with my life—write.

—Ahmed Faiyaz

PROLOGUE

In Mumbai
4 October 2009

It wasn't the most pleasant day to be flying out of the country. There was a storm brewing outside and most roads were flooded. If it wasn't as early as 4 a.m., Aditya would never have made it to the airport in time. It had been pouring steadily since early evening the previous day and the sky wore a purple-black shade, thundering threateningly. The taxi managed to navigate through water-clogged streets and dropped him off at Terminal C just an hour and a half before the scheduled departure time. To add to this, there was a security alert at the International Airport and there were certainly more eyes watching everyone. Aditya managed to pick up his boarding pass and moved quickly towards the immigration counter to stand in queue. He pondered over the events that had unfolded days and weeks before this planned trip. He stood there wondering if he was doing the right thing. *Will I get another chance?*

'Phew, why can't they just get on with it? We've been in this line for thirty minutes. Half the desks are empty with these guys taking long coffee breaks. When will our people change?' a voice behind him said.

He turned around and nodded in agreement. For a moment, he was taken aback. She was an attractive woman, not strikingly gorgeous like Ruheen, but attractive with an interesting face. She was tall and dusky with luscious lips and had this no-nonsense air about her. She wore her hair just like Ruheen did, and it struck him that what she said also sounded a lot like Ruheen. She wore a sleeveless cream top and a pair of figure-hugging grey jeans, and had a travel guide in her hand.

'Well, it's how these guys have always been,' Aditya said, averting his gaze from her.

'Yeah, well, it's time they change and become a little more efficient. I don't fancy standing around here while half of them decide not show up or are too busy drinking tea,' she said with a deep frown.

Aditya was called on next and had to answer the usual volley of questions that included 'baap ka naam?' before his passport was stamped. He walked ahead at a brisk pace towards the security check which, predictably, had a long line of frustrated and irate passengers who wanted nothing more than to board their flight and go to sleep.

At the check-in counter, more questions were being asked; hand baggage was being checked twice. He could see an elderly woman arguing with a burly security officer about his rationale for taking away her pair of pocket scissors. 'What harm will my pocket scissors do, baba?' he heard her saying to the big-built beefy Sardar who seemed apologetic and shook his head. The lady looked angry enough to want to snatch her pair of scissors from him. She thought better of it and walked away in a huff, muttering, 'nonsense' while another security officer smiled and nodded at the Sardar. Aditya picked up his backpack and walked towards the business class lounge with memories of Ruheen in his head.

He remembered the time when they flew in together to India—it seemed like it was yesterday. She seemed scared and wanted Aditya to hold her hand. She slept through most of the flight with her head on his shoulders. He remembered kissing her forehead and wrapping his arms around her which led her to snuggle closer to him.

'Sir, your flight is boarding now; you can proceed to Gate Number 12. Have a nice flight,' the waitress at the lounge said in a friendly voice.

Aditya finished his cup of coffee, picked up his backpack and walked towards Gate Number 12 feeling restless and unsure of the purpose of his trip. Would he meet her again? Would she be there?

Would I be able to hold her and run my fingers through her soft tresses? Would her hair be long the way I like it or has she cut it short like she always wanted to?

He boarded the flight and walked toward seat number 7B, searching for answers and remembering how miserable the last one and a half years had been. The years Ruheen and he had spent apart. The years Ruheen and he shouldn't have spent apart. He closed his tired eyes and tried to get these thoughts out of his disturbed mind.

We will be okay, he told himself.

'Excuse me, could you please move so that I can get in,' the annoyed girl from the line at the immigration counter said, tapping on his shoulders, stirring him from his deep reverie.

He sprang out of his seat, and moved out quickly to let her slide into 7A next to the window, a seat that he always preferred given the view from an aircraft taking off or landing in a city. He turned around and looked at her with searching eyes then, and now looked at her like he had seen a ghost. To her, Aditya certainly appeared to be lost in his thoughts and seemed disturbed about something.

She settled in quickly and wrapped a blanket around herself while he fiddled with the in-flight entertainment system. He began scrolling through the list of movies, looking for a movie to kill time. He gave up quickly and began reading from a worn, old diary.

He looked scruffy and it seemed to her that he had paid little attention to his own appearance. *He must be an independent writer, artist or a musician. He could also be one of those offbeat filmmakers,* she thought.

She felt that he was good-looking and had innocent eyes; it seemed like he was lost, like he was searching for something. He intrigued her and stood out from the usual band of boys who tried make small talk and used inane pick-up lines.

A short while after the aircraft had taken off for Brussels, she managed to accidently drop her hair clip which she was playing with while listening to Bruce Springsteen on her headset. It was below his seat and he bent down to pick it up while she removed the headset.

'Thanks!' she said, blushing in embarrassment.

'It's all right, here you go,' he said, handing it to her with a polite nod.

'Going to Brussels on work?' she asked, and then felt stupid as he certainly seemed like he wasn't. He could have been one of those guys going to Europe on a break to try and figure out what his life was about.

'No, I'm just transiting through Brussels. I have a flight to Amsterdam tonight,' he said, not really answering her question.

'That's a coincidence; I'm going to Amsterdam, too. It seems like we have a stopover of an hour or so...'

'An hour and thirty-five minutes, it will be past 9 by the time we reach Amsterdam,' he said in a pensive voice.

'I'm Meghna Sethi by the way. I am a talent manager and I represent a few young artists in India. I'm just going to Amsterdam for a couple of days, I have to strike this deal for Natasha Chopra's Europe Tour in a couple of months,' she said, observing that he didn't quite care what she did, that his mind was far away from the aircraft flying across the Arabian Sea.

'I'm Aditya Sharma, it's good to meet you,' he said, offering his hand to shake hers.

'So do you live in Mumbai?' she asked, sounding curious.

'In a way, yes I do. I have an apartment here but I've been away for almost a year.' He said this with rare honesty, and it now seemed like he wanted to talk to someone.

'Oh...you've moved recently much like I have. I live in Pune, moved like a year ago from Bangalore. It takes a while, adjusting to a new place, though both cities are quite similar in many ways.'

'Yes they are, except Bangalore gets a lot more rain,' he said with a reluctant smile, and added, 'it has Corner House, too.'

'Ha ha, yes we do. It's been our favourite place for a sundae from back in school!'

'Yes, I loved the apple pies there. I would head out to one of their outlets on every visit to Bangalore. Though coincidentally, each time I landed in Bangalore it was pouring like there was no tomorrow.'

'Welcome showers, I guess,' she said, reminiscing about the good old days.

'Yes, so they were. It was a good feeling to go there in summer and get away from the heat and humidity in Mumbai.'

'Yes, we have our summer showers to be proud of. I remember picking raw mangoes from the garden after the showers. Anyway, so who do you work with in Mumbai?'

'I'm not working with anyone at the moment,' he said, taking his gaze away from hers.

'Oh all right, so you're on a sabbatical from work or something?' she asked. She wondered if he was let go from where he worked.

'I quit a year ago, but that's not why I left Mumbai. I couldn't stand living there without her.'

'I see, without whom again?' she asked, not completely getting what he meant. She unbuckled her seat belt and put her feet up, turning almost completely towards him.

'Without Ruheen, my ex girlfriend...she's the reason I'm making this trip to Amsterdam. To possibly meet her and work things out,' he said with emotion in his voice.

'Well, I hope it all works out for both of you,' she said, touching his arm. He looked at her hand for a moment and nodded hopefully. 'Well it's a long shot but I'm trying,' he said, without much enthusiasm.

'Does she stay in Amsterdam?' she asked before realizing that she was being a little too inquisitive.

'She once did, it's where we fell in love. Or at least as I remember where she fell in love with me.' Anyone could sense the pathos in his voice and his longing for this woman.

'Tell me about it, when did this happen?' she asked with some interest wanting him to go on. It seemed to her like he could use a conversation. She felt this strange urge to want to know him, to hear his story and to figure out how someone could be so resilient and broken in love.

'Three years ago, in Amsterdam...' he stopped and stood up. He removed his backpack from the overhead cabin and took out an envelope containing photographs. He pulled one out and showed it to her. He had a faint smile on his face as he looked at the picture.

It was a picture of Aditya and a girl in a waitress's uniform in happier times. He had longer hair and his cheeks were full. He didn't have the dark circles under his eyes like he did now. The girl standing next to him had a broad smile on her face. She was petite and strikingly beautiful. She had sharp features, a tiny nose and a sexy pout; her light brown hair was tied in a bun and there was a warm glow about her. Her skirt and apron ensemble showed off nicely tanned legs. She was the kind of woman men would do anything for. She had that vulnerability in her eyes and a mischievous smile, one that could melt many hearts. One that could break someone's heart, it seemed to Meghna.

■

A few hours later...in Delhi

'I really like this cardigan for him. He will certainly look dashing in it,' Ruheen said, holding up the full-sleeved cardigan for her friend Priya to see.

'Hmm, it's not bad. But not too great either. Why don't we look elsewhere? There are other stores in Khan Market which will give it to you cheaper,' Priya said.

'I don't really care for cheaper. I want to see the look of surprise on his face when he sees this in a couple of days,' Ruheen said with a smile. 'Pack kar do, bhaiya,' she added.

'You might want to take something warm for yourself as well. It's a long trip, and it's certainly likely to be a lot cooler out there,' Priya said.

'Great idea, you're right, it will be cooler. I still can't believe I'm going to be doing this!' Ruheen said excitedly.

'You are doing the right thing. It's going to be another chance to build a new life for both of you,' said Priya, rummaging through the sweaters that were on display.

Her phone rang, it was Varun. 'Hi, you haven't left yet I gather?'

'No, I haven't, it's been crazy making all the arrangements. I'll leave now and I'll see you soon,' he said, sounding rushed.

'Okay, see you soon. Drive safely…'

■

At the same time…in Shimla

Varun walked into his office, animatedly discussing plans and ideas for the days ahead with a friend. Ruheen would be waiting for him. He should have left by now, but was unable to, given all the preparations that were underway.

'I have so much to wrap up before I take off for Delhi,' he said. 'Ruheen is the smart one, she wound up work a week ago.'

A member of his staff walked in and waited for him to finish his conversation.

'Shastri, I want you to pay close attention to the ongoing wedding preparations. Follow up with stage decorators and caterers and make sure they deliver as promised. Also make sure enough rooms are available for guests. We are expecting people from all over the place,' Varun said, looking at a missed call on his BlackBerry.

'I think the contractor is here. I'm going up to the Haveli

to coordinate some work that needs to be done. If Mishra comes here, send him down to the Oberoi Haveli.'

He picked up his keys and walked out to the car park in a rush. So *much to do and so little time,* he thought. *Let me call Ruheen and tell her that I'm leaving late.*

PART I

Finding Each Other
2003–2006

'What is the past, after all, but a vast sheet of darkness in which a few moments, picked apparently at random, shine?'
—JOHN UPDIKE *(Pigeon Feathers)*

In Mumbai
Six years ago…
Ruheen and Aditya crossed paths at Pizza Delight near where they lived, while back in college. He saw her at the takeaway counter one evening. He had seen her many times before, in college, at the cinema nearby, at Coffee Planet with her group of friends, which included a hefty monstrous-looking guy whom his group of friends had nicknamed Ogre. They each knew who the other was considering that they went to the same college and had hung out at the same café every day for the past two years. She was gorgeous, and for long he had intended to strike up a conversation with her. But it was something he could never get himself to do. He found her beauty to be intimidating.

'Hi, so you're picking up a pizza for a study night with your friends, huh?' Aditya asked, mustering up the courage finally. She turned around and looked, at him with a sparkle in her eyes, amused by his comment and his attempt to strike up a conversation. In his friends' circle, she was known to be the most beautiful girl in college. One whom half the college dreamed about going out with, but didn't have the guts to ask.

She turned towards him and looked at him with surprise and a glimmer of mischief in her eyes. 'Aditya Sharma, the super-intelligent MBA dude who lives down the street! So you finally had the guts to say more than "hi". Is there a bet among your friends that I'm unaware of? Do I intimidate you?' she asked teasingly.

'Ha ha, no, Ruheen you don't! But your boyfriend probably does intimidate a lot of people, not just me but every guy in college.' She was known to be a party animal and a bohemian babe who meant trouble, the type that guys like Aditya stayed away from generally. She made rare appearances in college and was more often seen at Coffee Planet sipping coffee and smoking Marlboro Lights with her ilk.

'Hai na? I knew this was the problem. But he isn't my boyfriend, dude! He just pretends he is, we've gone out just once,' she said with her sexy pout. She was wearing a loose sweatshirt and a pair of track pants. 'Where are you off to with a bag at this time? Didn't know that you guys went to classes at night—I barely manage to attend lectures during the day. By the time I wake up, get dressed and get to college, we're done for the day.'

'Well, lucky you. We have to endure a lot more than you do. Anyway, I'm just meeting a couple of guys to study decision trees. We'll sit and work out some problems together.'

'You seem like you study really hard. Is that what you do at the café? I always see your nose in a book or typing away on your laptop. Or are you playing games?' she asked with a seductive smile.

'Ha ha, well sometimes, not all the time. I'm working on assignments most of the time. Coffee Planet has air-conditioning, my room doesn't.'

'Why don't we cancel these pizza orders and go there? I feel like having a cup of coffee,' she said.

'Like right now? My friends are waiting to study.'

'Yes, like now! Stop making excuses, Ganesh will have the pizzas delivered, the one for my flatmates and the ones for your friends. Give him the address and let's go,' she said, puffing on her cigarette. Aditya called Mohan, his roommate, and told him that he was meeting a friend for coffee and would be home late. He hung up before Mohan asked any more questions.

They walked across to Coffee Planet and placed their orders at the counter. The barista was surprised to see the two of them together. It was the pairing of the most serious patron at the café who requested for the volume to be turned down and the girl who only left when the café would shut for the day at 2 a.m. She ordered an iced frappe while he stuck to his usual latte.

'I love this song,' she gushed.

'"With or without you"…yeah, it's one of my favourites.'

'Mine too,' she said with a smile, gazing at him intently as they both sipped cups of coffee they ordered.

They talked for a long time, she spoke about her school life, losing her parents at a young age, growing up in Shimla and about the books they had read, movies they had seen and music they loved. In all these respects they realized that they had similar tastes; they also had been through similar situations in life, she lost her parents as a child in a plane crash and he lost his parents, one after another as a result of chronic illnesses when he was a teenager. They got along like a house on fire and chatted for hours on end, till they were asked to leave when the café was shutting down. He walked her back home after a long chat and a few cups of coffee.

'My friends are out partying at Red Light with their boyfriends—they were here watching a movie before that. Thank God I got away to spend some time with you—it felt like a breath of fresh air, getting away from the usual crowd. Why don't you come up for a bit?'

Aditya followed her up with a nod of his head. He couldn't believe his luck. It had taken him two years to strike up a conversation with the girl of his dreams and now he was being invited up to her apartment. They carried the half-eaten pizza to the balcony and settled in to enjoy a view of the sea. Quite obviously, she and her friends were from affluent families to afford to rent an apartment by the sea.

'I'm so happy Vishal has left the city,' she said taking a bite of the pizza.

'Vishal the Ogre?' he asked with a grin.

'Ha ha, yes, him! He's such a psychopath; I had to complain

to the dean and then the cops to stop him from harassing me. I've changed my number thrice in the past one month; he would call a 100 times in a day.' She removed a pack of cigarettes and lit up. 'First he would moan and plead about how much he misses me and that we should be together. Then he would start abusing me, he would call my flatmates and abuse them. When he raised his hand on me, I went to the cops. His dad has called him back to Chandigarh now, I wonder if he is going to finish college. It isn't like he cares really!'

'That's crazy, what made you go out with a guy like that in the first place?'

'*Pata nahi,* he was quite sweet to start with. He treated me well, we had a good time partying in a group and he coaxed me to go out on a date with him. I've had trouble since—he started stalking me after I told him I don't see him and me working out,' she said with some irritation.

'Surprising, isn't it?' he said with some sarcasm while she looked at him, waiting for him to continue. 'You have to see it coming with people like him. One look at him and you know that he means trouble.'

'Appearances can be deceptive, Mr Wise Guy, who would look at you and think that you are not a geek?' She laughed at him with a cackle in her voice and said, 'Sorry, couldn't help that. That's what my friends call you. But I think you are pretty interesting.'

'Is that so? Why don't I pick you up and take you for a nice movie tomorrow night? We could go for dinner at Aurus after that,' he blurted that out, knowing full well that he would need to spend all his savings to afford dinner at Aurus.

'I don't know! I've had more than my share of trouble in the past few months. Weren't you seeing someone? I thought you were going steady with that slightly chubby girl with glasses who seems a little bossy?'

'You mean Vidya? We broke up two months ago. Come on,

it'll be fun,' he said, smiling persuasively.

'Sure, pick me up at 5 p.m. then, I'll figure out a nice movie to go to. Hey, I don't have your number, here store it on my phone and give yourself a missed call,' she said with a yawn.

'Sure, let's call it a night, I'll see you tomorrow,' he said, getting up to leave. He gave her an awkward hug; the touch of her skin felt soft. The smell of her hair was intoxicating and he realized how delicate she was. She put her arms around his neck and drew him close. Closing her eyes, she kissed him softly on his lips. They stood there, kissing in her balcony for a while—he was taken aback initially, but he cupped her cheeks in his palms and drew her lips into his. 'I always wondered what it would be like to kiss someone like you,' he said.

'Now you know,' she said, turning a shade of red and added, 'Goodnight, genius, dream about me!'

He walked back home at 3 a.m., feeling dizzy, and went up to his room. Mohan woke up to open the door for him. Aditya, still looking dazed, sat down on his single bed and told him excitedly where he was and who he had spent the evening with.

'Dude, Ruheen Oberoi! She's a goddess—*yaar,* you're going to flunk your exams!'

Aditya ignored his comment; it felt like he was on another planet. He could see Mohan looking at him with envy for going out with Ruheen Oberoi. He envied Aditya's luck with the fairer sex, and wondered why his own chances with them never worked in his favour. Aditya turned his attention to his phone which was vibrating; it was a message from Ruheen. They spent the rest of the night sending each other text messages. He finally managed to sleep at 5 a.m. and was woken up by Mohan at 8. 'Dreaming about your hot girlfriend? College *nahi jaana kya, yaar,* you're not coming to college?'

Later that day, Ruheen and he went out for an animated film which they saw very little of. They sat in the last row of the near empty theatre making out. He took her to Aurus for a relaxed dinner with a view of the sea. Later they went back to her place and cuddled on her couch, recreating the magic of that first kiss. She began coming to college more often and they often spent time together at the college canteen, where she would sit and drink coffee or smoke while he worked on assignments with the gang.

Ruheen and he would go back to her place from college together and he more or less began staying with her in her room. Mohan was going crazy seeing what Aditya was up to. He felt that if he had gone to pick up the pizza that night, he would be in Aditya's position right now.

■

A few weeks later, after he sang a karaoke version of 'With or Without You' for her at Not Just Jazz by the Bay, they made love for the first time on the heap of clothes on her messy bed. He ran his tongue all over her luscious body, holding her and whispering how much he wanted her. He entered her slowly, while she closed her eyes and guided him in, wrapping her arms around his waist. She moaned with pleasure and dug her fingernails into his back when she climaxed. They managed to do it twice in the same night, this time with her doing all the work. She made him gasp with pleasure and he was aroused with the warm touch of her skin and the way he felt with her body intertwined with his. He had never felt this way before—with Vidya, sex was a chore and it felt mundane. It was something they did like the assignments, something they got done with and moved on.

'I start my job with SK Products in June; I'm planning on taking an apartment in Juhu. Are you going to be in Mumbai as well?' he asked kissing her bare back with one hand cupping her firm breast.

She gazed at him with intense eyes, 'Why would I want to go back to Shimla, Adi? My Nana has enough money to support me; I feel most of the girls will continue to stay on in Mumbai, so I think we'll stay here and keep this apartment,' she said before snuggling closer and kissing him on his neck.

∎

A few weeks later
Ruheen and Aditya were sitting in the college canteen and having lunch. They ate quickly while he was explaining company law and contracts to her. What had started as a fling was now heading towards something more serious. They were spending a lot of time together. She had begun taking her studies seriously and would bring her books along while he studied or worked on assignments with the boys. However, it needed some cajoling and favours in the bedroom for her to give it some serious attention. She suddenly put her hand on his and tugged on his sleeve. He looked up from the book to see what she was staring at with an open mouth. A group of students were standing around them, some from her class and some from his. Standing right in front of them was Vishal the Ogre.

'Hi, Ruheen,' he said sweetly. 'So Mr MBA, the hotshot guy with a big job offer and a promising pay package. I hear you've been sleeping with my girlfriend while I was away. Why would an intelligent guy like you do something so stupid?'

Aditya looked at him with disdain while Ruheen looked at him with fear in her eyes. 'Please leave him out of this, Vishal, and for heaven's sake please leave us alone! I will go back to the police station if you don't stop—don't make me.'

'Do whatever you like, I don't care! I'll leave you alone, but I don't want to see this guy around you.'

'You can't walk around threatening people. Why don't you leave Ruheen alone, huh?' Aditya said firmly.

'*Acha,* is that so?' He knocked down the table and charged towards Aditya, while Aditya leaned ahead and swung a punch which landed on his jaw. Soon punches were flying and people around them were pulling the two of them apart. Aditya could see Ruheen standing there and looking on helplessly with tears running down her cheeks.

Her friends took her home; while his sat him down for some hardheaded advice.

'Dude, are you crazy? Are you trying to get yourself killed? Why are you getting in the way of this guy? It's her fault to have gone out with him in the first place. Focus on your course, man, don't ruin the life and opportunity you have before you,' Mohan said, sounding practical and many others nodded along.

'Do you want me to sit around and watch him mess around with her? She's my girl, man, she's with me. I have to look out for her!'

'Right now, he isn't doing anything to her, his problem is with you. He can't stomach the fact that Ruheen is with another guy. The bunch of goons he hangs out with have probably filled his head with stories—they're laughing at him,' Mohan said.

'Ruheen was bound to bring you trouble, man. We told you in the beginning. Why did she have to hang out with a guy like that Vishal in the first place?' Anil said.

'I have feelings for her, guys, get it? How often do you see me coming to blows in the canteen?'

'Yes, you're stooping to his level. You're an MBA student, he is riffraff. He is fighting for his ego and he has nothing to lose. You on the other hand, have a lot to lose, take it easy. Just let things be, once college is done with, we'll sort it out. You've just been with her for a month, it's a fling, don't go crazy at this stage. We have exams in a month,' Mohan said wisely.

'Well all right, let me think about it. I'm going over to her place to see if she is okay,' he said, walking out. He rode down to her building and saw his books and clothes lying on the street outside her building. She was crying in the balcony, and he ran up to her apartment.

'The police have taken him away, but I know he'll be out in a day or two, Adi,' she said, controlling herself. 'Just stay away from me, Adi, I don't want anything happening to you. He came in here and vandalized the place. He started throwing all your things out of the window and was muttering about how he is going to break your neck and knock your teeth out.'

'Bullshit, let him try,' Aditya said defiantly.

'I know what he is capable of, please just leave! Go away and don't try and speak to me, at least for a few days,' she said looking at him pleadingly. He couldn't bear to see her that way and walked down to collect his things from the street.

Ruheen attended very little of college. He stopped going over to Coffee Planet after college, not wanting to bump into her. Mohan did mention that he saw her there a few times looking confused and scared. He tried calling her after a week and Vishal picked up the phone. He had taken away her handset. He hurled a volley of abuses and called over thirty times that night from her phone, warning Aditya to stay away from her.

A few hours after her last exam, Ruheen flew out of Mumbai without saying goodbye.

Two months later...

Ruheen boarded the flight reluctantly, half wishing that she didn't have to leave. She typed a message to Aditya, trying to explain the reason for her leaving like this. She wished that life wasn't so unfair, and she didn't want to end things with him, at least not like this. The flight attendant asked her to switch off her mobile phone, which she did without sending the message.

She remembered the MMS clips Vishal had sent a week back, during the exams. He sent her clips of Aditya for three days in a row, showing him walking back from college or going for dinner at Ramu's Dhaba near college. She was frightened by these clips, even if she didn't understand them, she knew that Aditya was being watched. She felt relieved that she ignored him when he walked up to her in college every day after the exam and tried to talk to her.

A day after these clips, she received another disturbing MMS from an unknown number. The clip showed someone with the face hidden wringing the neck of a stray cat and throwing the limp body in a garbage bin. She threw up on seeing this, and wanted to call the police. She tried calling the number, but the line was disconnected.

With hot tears rolling down her cheek, in a fit of rage she dialled Vishal's number.

'*Haan meri jaan?* How was your accounting paper?' he asked.

'You bastard, what did you do? You are sick! You horrible...'

'Shut up! I haven't done anything yet. But if you want that chutiya to stay alive and not end up like that poor cat, you need to promise me something.'

'What is that?' she asked, her voice quivering with fear.

'Leave this city as soon as the exams are over. Do not try contacting this Aditya and ignore him if he calls you. Also, my driver will be there in ten minutes; give him your Sim card, he'll give you another one to use. Do you hear me?' he said in an intimidating tone.

'Yes,' she said reluctantly, hanging up with a look of agony on her face, before burying her face in her pillow and crying.

■

After spending a few weeks in Shimla, Ruheen moved to Delhi on the pretext of studying further or finding a job. She had cousins and school friends there and decided to stay with them, till she figured out what she wanted in life. She had felt extremely lonely in Shimla, and spent the waking hours wondering what her life could have been with Aditya.

Moving to Delhi raised her spirits. She had a number of people she could hang out with and she loved the cultural scene with books and film festivals, theatre, fashion shows and the nightlife. Life in Delhi mainly revolved around partying and shopping. She would wake up at noon, to go out and shop every evening before heading out for a night about town. Ruheen saw many men during this phase, but did little to take things forward with anyone, wary of trusting anyone given her experience with Vishal. She knew what the lads in Delhi were out to get, and she also knew what she wanted for herself. So yes, there was a lot of harmless flirting and dinner dates with people she had gotten to know. Ruheen was twenty-two and naïve; she did enjoy the attention being showered on her. It was the only way to get over her doomed relationship with Aditya.

After a few months of the good times in Delhi, she realized that most of her school friends had begun to move in different directions. Many got jobs, some got steady boyfriends. Then she went back to Shimla to visit her Nana, who was also funding her easy-come-easy-go lifestyle.

On getting there, Ruheen was in for a shock. Her Nana was ready and waiting to confront her about what she was up to after college. He had managed to get her marksheet from college which showed that she had failed miserably; whereas she had led him to believe a few months ago that she finished with a first class with honours.

Her Nana had decided to get her married off to Varun Shetty, his friend's grandson who lived in the US. Varun's dad, who had grown up in Shimla, ran a big logistics and distribution business in Bangalore and Varun, having just finished business school, had come back home and had joined the family business. Ruheen had known him many years ago, and remembered playing with him as a child.

'But Nana, I'm too young to get married! Maybe we can talk about this after a couple of years, okay? I'm working towards becoming a stylist for a fashion magazine in Delhi. I'm talking to a few people in the business and I should have a nice job in a few months. Please Nana, please!' she pleaded, trying to sweet talk her way out of the situation.

'No, please listen to me, Guddi. I am your guardian; you will have to listen to me and not argue. I'm worried about you and the life you've been leading, *beti*. The things you've done in the last eight years make me cringe. You wouldn't have ended up like this if your parents were around. I've spoiled you, listening to your every wish...' he said, coughing violently.

'Nana, relax, the doctor says you have to take it easy. There is no need to get agitated. I'm saying it's a little too early for me to be considering...'

'These are good people, I want you to stay here for the next six months, finish your backlog of subjects you failed in, and get married to this boy. You know Varun, don't you? You've met him many years ago in Shimla. Bangalore *mein apni zindagi bana,* live happily ever after. I remember both of you being very fond of each other,' he said with a broad smile.

'Nana, that was ages ago! People don't get hitched like this today, *aise thode hi hota hai…'*

'Guddi please, it's either this or you can forget that your Nana is alive!' he pleaded. He had tears in eyes and seemed very weak and vulnerable.

Ruheen remembered the time when he came and took her away from school in Bangalore, when her mum and dad died in a plane crash in Bangalore in 1988. She was seven years old then. She remembered how he would carry her on his back, take her for long drives to buy her ice cream and walk her to school every day. Her Nana never made her feel that she was less fortunate than any other child around her. While growing up, she realized that she took advantage of it and used his affection to get whatever her heart pleased. She remembered his first heart attack when she was expelled from school in class eleven.

'Okay Nana, I'll do whatever you want, please don't get upset like this!' she said, giving him a hug. But I'm going to spend a month in Delhi and then come here. I need to say goodbye to my friends and my life back there.'

'*Badmash!*' he said, giving her a hug.

The next month was a wild ride in Delhi. Ruheen partied and shopped to her heart's content.

She then put off moving back to Shimla, and kept buying time from her Nana, one month after another.

■

Meanwhile…

Aditya walked into the VS Distributors office; it was his third month on the job and he had been given the task of studying how to improve the distribution system of SK Products in Bangalore. He had a six-month assignment in this city and the management was pinning its hopes on him to help improve distribution and lower costs. VS Distributors was the company's oldest distributor in the city, and covered the busy and most prominent neighbourhoods of central Bangalore. The office was in a lane, behind the fish market of the busy Russell Market area. He couldn't believe that this was where he would need to come every day for the next few months. The overpowering odour made him want to retch, and he asked to be shown to the restroom.

He felt forlorn and didn't quite have his mind at work, despite being identified as the top management trainee during the training courses they had been put through. Although it was a lucrative market that was growing given the rise and rise of Bangalore, SK Products had seen no real growth in sales over the past couple of years. He was here to identify the sales and distribution problems at SK Products.

Aditya waited in the manager's cabin, which like the rest of the building had deep cracks on the wall, desperately needing a coat of paint. He had his mind still on Ruheen and how she had left without a word. He couldn't come to terms with the fact that she could just leave Mumbai without saying goodbye. He tried to get her home number in Shimla, but the college friends didn't have it, nor did they seem to care. They put him off coolly, saying that they would get in touch with him if they heard from her.

He sat back, thinking about her, and wondered where she was and what might have become of her. He thought about the last time he saw her. She had worn a pink sweater and light blue jeans, with her hair pulled back and her face pale as death. She had looked through him and walked away with a worried look on her face as he tried to ask her how she had fared in her exam.

He realized that he had been waiting for the past hour with no sign of the manager. On asking the staff, he was asked to wait a few more minutes. They seemed to be clearly irritated by his presence. A guy who seemed like an attendant, and who had brought him coffee earlier, was busy chatting online using the fake alias of john_abraham as well as using the actor's picture as his own. The receptionist was busy giggling on the phone on what certainly didn't seem like a business call. He also saw a few others, presumably salesmen and delivery boys who eyed him suspiciously; they certainly didn't like the city slicker in his Louis Philippe shirt and Zodiac tie.

An hour later, a tall, droopy-eyed, slightly chubby guy, with an air of authority walked into the cabin. He was casually dressed in a polo tee and a pair of casual cargos. He didn't seem much older than Aditya.

'Good morning, I'm Varun Shetty. I run this circus. Sorry I'm late, man, you've been waiting for a while huh?' he said with a friendly smile.

'Aditya Sharma, management trainee from SK Products. Yes, I believe we had set up a time for 9 a.m.'

'Did we? I presume we did. I was at this wild party last night, and I have a bit of a hangover. Sorry, man, I normally get here at this time, around 11 a.m. I don't see the point of getting here earlier than that. In the same way as I don't see the point of selling *tel malish* and such to kirana stores, after an MBA in Finance at Berkeley. Anyway, tell me, how can I help?'

'So how did you end up as a manager for a local distributor? With your degree, you certainly have better options,' Aditya asked, puzzled.

'You know, the old sign on the door needs to be changed. The manager was slain by one of our former van drivers. They got into a scrap over something. We haven't had a manager after that. No one really wants to manage our unruly bunch. I'm the Director of VS Distributors, the son of Vikas Shetty—he owns this dump. My brother in the office next door runs VS General Products.'

'That's well, quite shocking and unexpected. What I would

like to do is, go out into the market and study the order booking and delivery processes over the next few days.'

'Sure, Deepak will go with you today to cover the Jaymahal area. He can take you into Cooke Town tomorrow. One thing, don't let any of these guys know where you stay,' Varun said.

'Okay...what?'

'Ha ha, chill. I'm just kidding! How do you like Bangalore? There's a party at Bangalore Club tonight. Why don't you come along? You can meet a few people, hang out and relax.'

'Thanks, maybe some other time, Mr Shetty. I have reports to send out to my project manager back in Mumbai.'

'Boy, you're one of those serious ones, aren't you? Call me Varun, that'll do. Bakshi, your Sales Director, often comes to Bangalore. Half the time he's getting drunk at the Taj or Bangalore Club with my dad. That pretty much is what his sales visits are about,' Varun said with a wry grin.

'I didn't know that,' Aditya said feeling awkward hearing these stories about the senior management in the company.

'Aye Deepak, where the fuck are you? *Saala haraamkhor!* You don't get paid for showing up at 11 a.m. *chutiya!* I need you to take the manager from SK Products on a market visit. I also need you to run a sales report by the end of day. Make sure that you're here in ten minutes,' Varun barked on the phone. 'Bastard, pick up a pack of Marlboro Lights on your way here.'

'Sorry, man, this guy is a distant relative. Takes advantage of the fact that he's related to my dad. If it were up to me I would fire him tomorrow. Tea? Coffee? Cigarettes?' he asked.

'A cup of tea, thanks,' Aditya said while Varun lit up.

'There's another *kaamchor* sitting outside and chatting with women from Brazil,' he said with a disgusted look on his face and picked up the hand phone, 'Jyothi, why is your line busy all the time? Ask that idiot Satish to bring us two cups of tea. Also get him off Deepak's computer now.'

'Why don't you take it easy today? You could come with me to the Club this afternoon. We can have lunch there and play some snooker, have a drink or two, and you can always start tomorrow. That *chutiya* Deepak won't be here till after 1 p.m. It will be too late to go to the market, order booking finishes by 2 p.m.'

'Are you sure? I really need to get started, Varun.'

'Yes, yes don't worry. You can begin tomorrow, I'll make sure Deepak's here by 8 a.m. Or else, I'll be happy to fire him or send him away to one of my dad's other prosperous enterprises.'

Aditya sat back shrugging his shoulders. Once again his thoughts went back to where Ruheen might be and who could have been with her.

3

Eight months later...

Ruheen ended up breaking the promise made to her Nana. While partying with the girls one night at Code Red, Ruheen was introduced to Rohan Aluwalia, an NRI brat from London. Rohan was visiting family in Delhi and they ended up spending a lot of time together, at a friend's farmhouse near Delhi. They headed out to parties every night, Rohan practically shifted from his Bua's into her little room, and they shacked up together. Ruheen found herself drawn towards Rohan; he was cultured and well bred unlike most guys she had met in Delhi, who began mentally undressing her before even knowing her name.

One night, at a party in Liquid Lounge, Ruheen saw Vishal in an inebriated state, walking up to her with a wicked grin on his face.

'So, Memsahib, where is that geeky boyfriend of yours? *Darr ke mare mar gaya kya?*' He gazed at her with lust, setting his eyes on her shapely figure. She immediately regretted having worn a revealing party dress.

'Stop bothering me! I thought you had left the country.'

'I came back for a holiday. *Kyun,* not allowed, *kya?* Come on, babe, let's dance,' he said, taking her forcefully by her arm and dragging her towards the dance floor. He ignored her pleas to leave her alone.

A few seconds later, he felt a tap on his shoulder. 'I felt her message is loud and clear, yeah? Get your paws off the lady,' Rohan said, staring at him in the eyes.

'*Oye,* get lost. You're from *Amreka* or *Kenada, kya?* Do you know who I am? *Tu* regret *karega, chal* leave us alone,' Vishal said gruffly. 'This chick is mine.'

In a flash Rohan was upon him, striking him in the face with a left jab followed by a right hook. He picked up a half-empty bottle of beer from a window sill, and smashed it on Vishal's head, causing a deep cut on his forehead. Vishal could do little but swing his arms without purpose, failing to connect any of his attempts to strike Rohan. The bouncers rushed in and separated the two, asking both of them and their friends to leave the lounge. A scared Vishal staggered out with one hand on his forehead and the other on the arm of a friend. He winced in pain, and looked at his bloody hand and the dripping blood from his forehead with shock and worry.

'Thanks, for stepping up. I was scared to death out there,' Ruheen said to Rohan in the car, on their way back home.

'No worries, I'm always there to protect you, yeah?' he said in a charming voice and with one hand stroked her cheek. 'There is nothing you should worry about. My dad's friend is a minister in the city. I'll call him tomorrow morning and see how we can keep that fool at bay.'

'I'm tired of all this. These guys and their regressive behaviour towards women—I'm so glad I met you.'

'Hmmm, I get what you're saying. You need a change of scene. You should think about moving to London.'

'Well that's something to think about,' she said in a contemplative voice. She didn't want to rush into a commitment with him, but didn't want to lose him either, knowing that he was on a break and was to return home in a few weeks.

After a few weeks of bliss, Rohan asked her to marry him. It was the reason why he was in Delhi in the first place. His family had sent him here to see girls, and in Ruheen he had found the person he wanted to be with.

Faced with a difficult choice, Ruheen called Nana and told

him about Rohan's proposal. He was heartbroken and pleaded for her to come back home and not do this.

'I am doing this, Nana. I want to marry him and live in London,' she said firmly.

'I beg you not to do this, Guddi! We don't even know these people. Indians in London are very different...'

'Nana, please, this is my final decision! We plan to get married in Goa, please come for the wedding. Come to Delhi, and we can fly to Goa together. I need you to be there.'

'I don't approve of this wedding. I don't know these people, how can I give you away like this! How can the family not approach me and ask for my permission?'

'Nana, relax! Forget all these old school customs.'

'Guddi, please listen to me! Everything that is mine is yours, and it always will be. Don't marry Varun if you don't have to. Marry someone else, somebody that is more suited...'

'Nana, my decision is made. The wedding is in a few weeks. I want you to come,' she said firmly.

'I definitely won't be there! You forget that your grandfather is alive, *beti*,' he said in an agitated voice before hanging up.

Ruheen tried calling a number of times but the servants were ordered not to pass on her call. A couple of Nana's friends in Delhi tried to intervene, and advised her to listen to her old grandfather. But Ruheen was in no mood to listen. She was angry with her grandfather and believed he was trying to dictate her life. She began to dream of a blissful life in London with Rohan, and had no time to think about anything or anyone else.

A few weeks later, Rohan and she had a small wedding in Goa. Delhi was too cold for their taste and Goa also gave Rohan's family and friends from the UK an opportunity to take a beach holiday.

Rohan seemed all right to her during the wedding celebrations, though he was rakish and a bit arrogant in his attitude. Ruheen believed that growing up in the environment that he did was the cause. She felt there was a clash of cultures and a lot of confusion in the minds of youngsters from South Asia who grew up in London. He spoke little about work, and while in Goa, they rented a bike and took off on trips to different beaches every day. They ended up partying a lot and even got each other's names tattooed on their arms.

All in all, he seemed like Ruheen's kind of guy and marriage to her didn't seem like such a bad thing. His mother even assured her that she could study fashion design and work somewhere in London. They took a short trip to Spain for their honeymoon, where they continued to drink and party before they went to London to start their lives together.

■

Meanwhile…
Aditya was sitting in front of a large screen watching a competitive game between Arsenal versus Chelsea with a group of other youngsters. Most of them were hardcore fans, sporting jerseys of one or the other team; he noticed them heckling and cursing each other and players on the screen, getting completely into the game. He had only seen this kind of fan following and competitiveness during an India versus Pakistan cricket match. He didn't care too much for football and for some reason he found himself feeling completely out of place. He didn't care if Henry scored and Lampard didn't. Most of the others around him had been to college abroad and had known each other for ages. Everyone was getting wasted; the DJ playing music outside was winding up his unsuccessful gig. Some of the party animals were in the pool with their clothes on, telling the DJ to go on.

Aditya felt a tap on his shoulder.

'Can you move in?' a girl said in a husky voice. She wore a short grey dress, had barbed wire tattooed on her arm and a cigarette between her lips.

'Sure,' he said making room for her and sliding in.

'Thanks, you a friend of Mickey's?' she asked with interest. 'I haven't seen you before,' she said, taking a puff and blowing smoke into his face.

'No, I came here with Varun. I'm from Mumbai, I work for SK Products.' He realized he had given her too much information.

'Aah, Varun, the Lothario. Where is he? I know, he's probably up in Mickey's room with Suman. Those two have been at it lately, copulating like bunnies. Mickey's my younger brother. I'm Smriti by the way. I just finished my Master's in English Literature at Manchester City College,' she said.

'Aditya Sharma,' he said, putting out his hand to shake hers.

'Do you much care for this game? Because I don't—let's go out by the pool, it's a lot calmer out there,' she said, picking up a bottle of beer and walking out. Aditya followed her out with his glass of whisky.

'So where did you go to college, Aditya?' she asked with a slur in her voice.

'Scindhia School of Business, I finished last year,' he said gazing at the stars, half lost in his thoughts.

'All right, that's a good school. A friend of mine from back in boarding school used to study there. Though she was in Scindhia School of Commerce and not the one you went to. I'm not sure if you know her—Ruheen Oberoi, brown hair, light brown eyes, very fair, really popular with the boys…'

'Ruheen Oberoi! The girl from Shimla?' Aditya asked with a start.

'Yes, we were together for a couple of years in Shimla, class eleven and twelve standard. We hung out quite a lot; she stayed with her grandfather and not in the hostel like me. How do you know her?' she asked casually.

'We dated briefly,' Aditya said with a faraway look, feeling a head rush.

'Oh poor you, you certainly don't look happy about it. It's a small world, man! I mean here I am, standing with the ex-boyfriend of the girl I used to sit with in school. Why did you break up?'

'Complicated situation, another guy who was obsessed about her got involved, and things got messy. Do you know where she is?'

'Typical Ruheen, guys would go nuts over her. I can see a crazy look in your eyes at the mention of her name. Till now you were busy admiring the moon,' she said with a laugh and added, 'No, I don't have a clue. I haven't heard from her for what, like a couple of years now,' she said, sizing up Aditya with interest.

Aditya felt a tug on his arm. 'Come on, we have to go,' Varun said, and added, 'Sorry, drag him away, we'll be back in bit, Smriti.'

'That's okay, see you later,' she said with friendly smile, and walked back towards the house with her drink in her hand.

They got into Varun's new Octavia and drove back towards the city. Varun turned up the volume, psychedelic trance blared over his Bose speakers. He seemed on the edge and drove rashly. He would certainly fail a breath test—it reeked of alcohol and he had possibly smoked marijuana as well. He had deep red marks on his neck, presumably hickies, from fooling around with Suman, his current squeeze.

'Where are we going, Varun?'

'Just to pick up some weed, dude. We've run out of it, Mickey and the rest really want some, and the supplier only gives it to me. It isn't too far man; we should be back at the farmhouse in thirty to forty minutes.'

'So Smriti Khanna, huh? Nice choice, I hear that she's moving to Mumbai to work in a publishing house. I could help with more information. I don't think she's dating anyone. Though you'll need to put yourself through reading her angst-ridden poetry,' Varun said with a laugh.

'No man, nothing like that. It's just that I went to college with someone who was with her in school,' Aditya said stoically.

'All that is okay, man. I could see interest in her eyes. Women like her, they like nice boys. You've heard of the opposites attract theory, right? Go for the kill dude…' Varun said with a sporting grin. He almost rammed into an autorickshaw while taking a sharp turn into a pitch dark gully, and muttered curses at the hapless autorickshaw driver.

Aditya sat back and thought about his life as Varun zipped through the poorly lit, pot-holed streets at manic speed. Here he the was picking up weed from a dope dealer, for a bunch of guys most of whom he had only just met, miles away from the woman whose memories he was haunted by. He wanted to get back and talk to Smriti, he wanted know more about Ruheen back in school; he wanted to learn more about her.

Once they got back, he walked around the farmhouse looking for Smriti, after turning down Varun's offer to sit down and smoke a joint with them. Smriti had left the party, and on asking around he was told that she was to leave for Mumbai in a couple of days.

4

Six months later...

After a few months of marital bliss, over the weeks and months that followed, Ruheen realized that things had gone horribly wrong. The weather in London was cold and damp, pretty much all through the year. She hated how gloomy it was and how depressing life was out there. Rohan and she had a room in his mum and dad's basement. He had two younger brothers and a sister who also lived in the same house. They lived in a middle income, Indian neighbourhood in Southall where there were drunken brawls and cases of people knifing each other for no reason every day. Rohan's dad ran a kabab shop on the same street and one in King's Cross which was managed by a guy who had worked for them for over twenty years. Rohan did little work apart from minding the shop for a few hours in the night. He sat at home and smoked all day or played games on his console.

Initially, Ruheen believed that Rohan was taking it easy as they were newly married, but the growing distance between them and the fact that Rohan was withdrawing into alcohol and drug abuse shocked her. On some evenings he went out with his group of buddies from the neighbourhood and came back wasted every single time.

His parents said nothing, they preferred to maintain a distance and let him be. The father lived in his own make-believe world, reminiscing about the days of his youth in India, back in the '70s. He also got worked up about racism and crime in London and about India going to the dogs. The mother did little beyond meeting other fat Indian women for tea, screaming occasionally at the younger kids and having heated debates with her daughter regarding the 'white boys' she went out with. Ruheen was confined to the kitchen and was responsible for making dinner for the entire family as well as keeping the house clean. She was also forbidden from wearing western attire or going out by herself, and often was subject to scathing comments on her appearance and her intention to find a job by her mother-in-law. '*Ram ram*, aren't you being fed and looked after?' or 'Yes, you also go and work and leave me to slog and put food on the table and clean this house! No sense of duty among people like you. I've been working like a slave for thirty years. This isn't like your grandfather's *kothi*, there are no *naukar chakar* in London!'

Rohan and she had begun to have arguments every day. Their love life was abysmal and Ruheen began to realize that she had married a train wreck. Rohan paid more attention to Grand Theft Auto or Need for Speed on his playstation, than his wife trying to seduce him in a sexy ensemble. Rohan, she realized, was an idiot in every respect; she knew that he had never really matured, living off an allowance which his mother gave him. He had failed to make it through college, he had been arrested and had served time for drunken brawls and was above all, a dope head.

One day he got back from the kabab shop in a blood-stained and torn shirt and his breath reeked of beer and cigarettes. Ruheen usually waited up for him, to serve him dinner.

'I've been waiting for the last couple of hours and you show up at midnight, drunk like a fish. Why are there blood stains on your shirt? What happened to your hand?' she asked, seeing that he was wincing with pain.

'Got into a fight, this bloke had the nerve to heckle me at the shop, calling me "curry breath" and "serve it faster Paki". I broke his nose with my fist. It would have been worse if the boys hadn't stopped me. You should have seen his face, all bloody and with tears running down his cheek,' he said with a deranged look in his eyes and laughing maniacally.

'Rohan, why do have to get into brawls all the time? Why are you like this? Some day things are going to get bad...'

'Shut up, shut up, you damn whore,' he said, slapping her hard, before grabbing her hair and pushing her against the wall. 'Do you want me to break your nose? Do ya?' She shook her head with fear, tasting blood from her cut lip, and tears running down her cheek.

'No, you wouldn't, would you? I thought as much, you wouldn't want me to wreck that pretty face of yours. Now get to bed, and get undressed, I'm coming there in ten minutes,' he said with a wicked grin, before pushing her across the room, and walking towards the refrigerator, looking for an ice-cube for his swollen knuckles.

He continued to assault her for asking him why he drank so much. This behaviour continued unchecked by his parents. He would either assault her or try to forcefully have sex every time he pleased, before he passed out. He sometimes muttered an apology the following morning, when he saw her with a swollen face or a black eye. His tyrant of a mother pretended nothing was wrong, believing that it was normal for a married couple to fight and would pass comments on how it was time for Ruheen to bear a child and start a family of their own.

■

After six months...

One evening Rohan's sister Shilpa, on the pretext of taking her to the doctor, took her out for a cup of coffee to Costas, near Handel House in Mayfair. It was a neighbourhood that her brother would stay away from, one which he despised and hurled abuses at every given opportunity.

'You know if you complain Rohan can be sent off to jail again? Why do you not say or do anything?' she asked, looking dismayed.

Ruheen began to sob—she thought about her Nana who called her every week to ask after her. She remembered his words on how she was making a mistake with Rohan before the ill-fated wedding.

'Did you know that Rohan was married before this, when he was nineteen? His ex-wife and his little boy live in Blackpool. My dad sends them an allowance that helps them get by. Rohan is trouble, I feel so bad to be a part of this...to see you put up with him.'

Ruheen was aghast and looked shocked by what she had heard. She could come to terms with the fact that he was a good-for-nothing loser who hung out with people such as himself and beat his wife every night but the revelation of a wife and kid from the past was something she couldn't imagine.

'She left him after he tried to kill her when she was pregnant. He went to jail for this and is restrained from seeing her or the kid. Anyway, do you even know why my parents got him married off to you?'

Ruheen shook her head with disgust, wanting to hear what this was about.

'They want your grandfather's property and money. Papa is broke; the shops aren't doing so well, we have a mortgage on the house, a good-for-nothing son and two boys in school. Rohan was sent to India with the intention to woo you and get married. It was a set up by my family and his friends in Chandigarh who knew about your family and your ancestral wealth. He feels it's a matter of time before the property passes on to you. He wants to sell or lease it to a friend of his who wants to build a hotel in Shimla. They've had this plan for many months. They convinced Rohan to go along with this; else they would turn him on to the streets. This is why I didn't come to your wedding, I'm really sorry...'

'You people put me through all this for my Nana's property? What gives you the right to ruin people's lives? What am I supposed to do? If my Nana finds out it's going to kill him! I've brought him nothing but misery all his life.'

Shilpa placed her hand on Ruheen's while she sobbed like a little girl.

'I'm sorry!' She gazed at Ruheen who looked forlorn. 'He

wasn't always like this you know. He was never good in studies, but was a good footballer. He lived to play centre forward for his school team. He dreamed to play for Liverpool. Papa was against it, and railed against him. Papa got him thrown off the junior league team to focus on studies. He never did, he got worse. He hung out with the wrong crowd—drinking, smoking, doing drugs, bar fights, vandalism…' Ruheen looked like she didn't want to hear any more about him. *How could I not see through all this? Despite seeing him go berserk at the bar in Delhi,* she thought.

'Why can't you just divorce Rohan and go back?'

'How can I? I've been the reason for my Nana's last heart attack. I can't do it, Shilpa,' she said tearfully.

'Okay, calm down. Look, we need to get you out from here. My boyfriend James owns a few businesses in Amsterdam. His family has cafés there and you can go and work at one of them. He'll take care of you. Don't worry about my family, they won't come after you. They'll try and find you but their resources are limited to the city. They won't tell your grandfather as they still would want his property and they wouldn't want to invite any trouble as he could go to the cops.'

'Why do I have to run away and live like a criminal? Why can't I go back to India?' Ruheen asked with fury in her eyes.

'You can't confront Rohan here; you know what he can do. My folks know people, and they have people back in India. They can easily come after you in India. Out here in London, they would be afraid as Rohan has a bit of history with the police and anything they might try in terms of tracking you down might put them in a spot of bother. Besides, if you try to leave or confront them here you never know what Rohan might do,' Shilpa said with a look of concern.

A chill passed through her spine. 'Yes, Rohan is very violent and unstable.'

'Exactly, he could attack you in a fit of rage! Besides, Europe is a continent; it will be very hard for him to track you down. Even if he does we can take care of it. We will make sure you are protected. From where I stand, they don't know who James is or my connection with this whole thing. I could arrange for you to disappear...'

'What about my Nana? If he knows any of this it could kill him,' Ruheen said, fearing the worst.

'He won't know, they won't let it get that far. They'll try looking for you here once they know that you're not back in India. If your Nana finds out, he might file a case against them and raise a ruckus. They wouldn't want that. They are very scared of the police out here. They'll wait for you to come back. With your Nana, you could play along and pretend that you're still out here, it's a matter of a few months or maybe a couple of years...'

'A few months or couple of years, till what? I'm not getting this clearly, Shilpa. Why do I have to seek asylum and live in another country?'

'Till Rohan's luck runs out. He's been in and out of rehabilitation. Eighteen months ago he was diagnosed with lung cancer and is undergoing treatment, though his chances of survival, given his lifestyle, are bleak. My folks hope to cash in on your grandfather's property before anything happens to him. I really doubt that, he's unlikely to survive...' she said this with some sadness for her sibling whose life was one of wrong choices and confusion. He had strayed onto the wrong path and things had only gotten worse. Ruheen didn't feel sorry for him.

Three weeks later, Ruheen with help from Shilpa and James fled to Amsterdam. They took a train to Paris, and soon after changed trains to Brussels. After a couple of nights in Brussels, to make sure that they were not followed, they took a train from Brussels to Amsterdam. Shilpa had managed to sneak Ruheen's passport out of her mother's cupboard and, with James' help, had managed to get Ruheen a work visa to leave the UK.

5

A year later...

Aditya was in Amsterdam for a business meeting with Zenith Cosmetics, which was headquartered in the city. He was now the marketing manager for SK Products Limited and was in Amsterdam to discuss a deal his company was to ink with Zenith Cosmetics. As a part of the deal Zenith were to bring their Enigma range of men's hair creams, styling gels and shaving products to the Indian market. SK Product's Shudh hair oil and Shakti range of hair creams were taking a beating in the market. Sales were stagnant and their bigger competitors were taking a huge chunk of the growing market. It was a battle to survive and the top management of SK Products comprising the CEO, CFO, Sales Director and Aditya had come to Amsterdam for a series of negotiations with Zenith.

After the successful conclusion of the deal, SK Product's CEO and CFO flew out to London to meet institutional investors and lenders to discuss funding needs for expansion and growth. The Sales Director, Mr Bakshi, and Aditya stayed back in Amsterdam for three more days, to unwind and take a brief holiday before they went back to India.

Mr Bakshi got busy enjoying some of the things Amsterdam was famous for—strip clubs, sex shops and smoking weed in cafés. For him it was an escape from the mundane world and he used the opportunity to make use of every moment away from his wife and kids. After the first day of following him around on his adventures, Aditya excused himself feigning fatigue, saying that he was much better off resting it out and reading a book at a café. He simply didn't have the appetite to watch Mr Bakshi take voyeuristic pleasure in everything that was around him.

He decided to explore the hauntingly beautiful city, leaving behind the sights he saw with Mr Bakshi the day before. It felt like he was suddenly a part of a fairytale. He took off on a long walk exploring the city on foot. He later took a cycle on rent and went on a nice ride through the Old Centre and by the canals. In the afternoon, he visited the Van Gogh Museum and the Ajax Museum, being a big fan of theirs back in school. In the evening he took a long boat ride, sitting back and taking in the history and culture around him. It was a blissful experience; a refreshing change from the traffic and chaos that he was used to. At the end of the day, he went back to the Old Centre area by train and walked towards his hotel—the Rho Amsterdam. On a sudden whim, he decided to visit a quaint coffee shop on the sidewalk called Fusion Café. A few moments later, a waitress was standing before him holding out the menu card.

'We also have a nice selection of teas and desserts if you would like. They are not on the menu but I could tell you what these are...'

'Ruheen!' Aditya said, looking up at her with surprise. She still looked stunning, but seemed a lot paler and mellower than the girl he once knew.

'Jasmine, my name is Jasmine!' she said in an agitated but desperate voice. She looked frightened and it seemed like she wanted to cut short and run. 'I'll send Desmond here to take your order,' she said softly, turning her gaze away from him. The badge on her apron said 'JASMINE', but Aditya couldn't be wrong. She had the same eyes, the build, her hair and that elegant pout. He would have recognized her anywhere and among any number of women. Given that she was very fair-skinned, she could pass off as European but her English accent was still very Indian, which gave her away.

'Ruheen, wait! It's me, Aditya Sharma from Scindhia College.

You still remember who I am, right? Look, it's okay, I'm just here on work.'

'How did you find me? Anyway, I can't talk now, Aditya! I'm on duty now,' she said self-consciously.

'Why don't we chat when you're done? I'll wait for you.'

She pondered for a moment and said, 'Why don't you hang around for about an hour and we could catch up when my shift is done? What can I get you now?'

'A tall latte and a cherry muffin—sure I'll wait for you to finish,' he said before she turned around and walked away with a nod of her head.

The coffee and muffin was served to him by Desmond who curtly asked if he needed anything else before he brought the check. It was past 9 p.m. but it was still bright outside, there was a lot of hustle bustle apart from the scent of weed in the air. Young couples, groups of friends and kids on a spring break from college moved about spiritedly towards wherever they were headed.

Before he got up to leave, Ruheen walked up towards him in a black top and black skirt looking depressingly gorgeous. She seemed guarded and in a businesslike manner said, 'Let's walk Aditya, not here. I work here. Let's go and get a drink.'

He walked across the promenade behind her, thinking about the days and months he had spent, wondering where she was and what had become of her. A picture of them, taken back in college, in happier days, was etched in his memory; all these years he had longed to return to those days and relive them.

6

Later that night…

Aditya and Ruheen walked into a nearby pub and sat outside to order a pitcher of Amstel Light, while Ruheen lit a cigarette. 'Do you want one?' she asked. 'It isn't a joint,' she added.

'No I don't smoke…'

'Just like the old days! So how have you been, Adi?' He liked the way she called him Adi. There was warmth and familiarity in her voice and she smiled at him cheerfully before taking another puff. She seemed to ease up a bit and let go of her fears.

'I'm all right, doing well at work. I was here to work out an important deal. It's been quite a while, something like three years since I last saw you. You moved out of Mumbai soon after the exams, if I remember correctly. How have you been?'

'Well, yeah, I did move out, we didn't have a chance to talk before I left. I'm sorry about what happened then. Anyway, look, my life has been all over the place since then…' She had a faraway look in her eyes and he locked his gaze with hers, wanting her to continue. He had many questions, how did she get here? *Why is she a waitress? Why does she go by the name of Jasmine?*

Ruheen began her story after a few moments of silence while she took long drags from her cigarette. Fixing her gaze on his, she began. She told him about her days in Shimla and Delhi, as well as the journey from getting married after an eight-week romance to living through marital abuse and her escape from London, a year ago. She didn't bring up the MMS clips from Vishal and his threats as she didn't want to alarm him.

'You've been through hell, Ruhi,' Aditya said in a pensive voice, putting his palm on hers.

'Well, much of it was my doing, I made some horrible choices. I've had to face the music and deal with what I've signed up for. I feel life is getting back at me for all the things I've done and all the mistakes I've made,' she said, turning her gaze to a couple who were kissing passionately at a table across the street, outside Bert's Café.

'I think you've been through more than your share of misery. How do you manage here, all by yourself ?'

'I've been here for eighteen months. Some days, I feel tired, alone and depressed...but it's better here. I don't live in an old English home which feels like India in the 1960s. I come and go as I please. I earn my own wages for the first time in my life; I pay my rent, my taxes and my bills. I don't get abused or beaten up. I've managed to stay sane and sorted in a place like this! I can't complain really, these eighteen months have taught me a lot about life,' she said cheerfully.

'You seem surprised. See, initially I was scared; I was a bundle of nerves. I watched my back a lot, it felt like Rohan was here and he was following me. I was living with fear; I felt danger was lurking around every corner. There were nights when I woke up and couldn't go back to sleep. One day, I called Shilpa telling her that I saw someone who looked like Rohan, and that I could sense his presence. She asked me to relax, Rohan was in a bad shape; he had been locked up for a month after a drunken brawl with a skinhead outside the kabab shop. I realized then, that this was fear within me. Either I could let go and embrace life, or live waiting to be caught by Rohan and taken back to London. I chose the former—if the worst happens I'll deal with it then, but I'm in a better place now,' she said gingerly.

'I'm glad to hear that, I can't believe it is really you, sitting here before me. I mean, imagine the likelihood of this happening...'

'Yes, it's a pleasant blast from the past. You're probably the only guy, among the few I've been in a relationship with, whom I would ever like to meet, the rest be damned.'

'Cheers to that,' Aditya said with a smile.

'I'm sorry about what happened with Vishal back in college. You know what my position was. I did have your number and a few months later I did want to call you. I was just too embarrassed to meet you or say anything then. You must have felt horrible when I left without saying goodbye,' she said, turning her gaze towards him.

He noticed how fragile and vulnerable she still was. *Some things never change*, he thought.

'It's okay, don't worry about it. That guy was a bloody maniac! You've been through enough drama in your life; besides it was a long time ago. How did you finally get rid of him?'

'I didn't, I went to Delhi and he went to join his father's new business in Australia. He was one crazy guy! I wonder why I end up with men like these. I keep walking into these traps. These are things one should be able to see through...'

'You were obviously very young when all this happened. You did end things with him when you figured out how he was,' he said, trying to make her sound like someone with good judgement.

'Yes, but not before the damage was done. He drove away the one really nice guy I met in college, and began to grow fond of...' She smiled at him sweetly, which made him return the smile. *Watch where you're headed,* he told himself, as they sat looking at creatures of the night walking to and from cafés and pubs near Dam Square.

■

Both of them sat at the café till midnight talking about her life in Delhi and afterwards, while Aditya spoke to her about life after college. He mostly spoke to her about work, his success and growth in the company. That's pretty much what he had to show for the three years—the rest of it was a blur.

'I better head back, Adi, it's quite late and I start work at 9 a.m. How long are you here for?' she asked, with those beautiful eyes looking deep into his.

'I leave the day after tomorrow. I have an early morning flight. Can I drop you in a cab? It's too late for you to go back home on your own.'

'Well, cabs are freaking expensive! This isn't Mumbai, Adi,' she said with a laugh. 'You can walk me to the station; it's a ten-minute walk. I stay in Jordaan, it's fifteen minutes away by train. This is a very small place.'

'Sure, let's go. Hey, I don't have your number. Is it okay for me to have it?' he asked. She gave him her mobile number with a strange smile, one which he couldn't fathom, while they kept walking.

'I remember what happened when I gave you my number last time,' she said with a sparkle in her eyes.

'I don't, not really, enlighten me,' he said playfully.

'Oh shut up, Adi, you kept texting me all night.'

'You kept texting back,' he said with a grin.

'You started,' she said, running her fingers through her tresses.

'That I did. I couldn't help myself, especially after you put your arms around me and leaned in. I thought you wanted to kiss me, didn't you?'

'So would you be coming here quite often?' she asked with interest, trying to change the subject.

'I'm not sure. Not too often, I suppose. Maybe initially, I will. So you stay all by yourself ? What do you do on a day off ?'

'I do stay by myself; I have a nice little loft by the canal. James' cousin stays a couple of buildings away. He manages the café I work at, and a couple of others. I don't have a day off; I take half days a couple of times during the week, when I feel like it. It's too depressing to stay in. Once a week I sleep till late and get to work in the evening and on another day, I get off work early. I go to the cinema or a bookstore. I get back early and take care of my laundry. It's a busy life...'

'It sure sounds busy—you do seem to have settled in,' he said rather eagerly.

'Yes, it isn't what I expected my life to be. Given that I have no expectations now, it isn't bad. It's a peaceful existence,' she said in a pensive voice while lighting up another cigarette as they approached the station across the street.

'So here we are—it seems like a lot of people take the train even at this hour,' he said, noticing streams of people walking towards and from the subway that was the entrance to the main station.

'Yes, they do. All right then, Adi, till the next time we are destined to meet again. Take care and enjoy the rest of your time in Amsterdam. Call me before you leave, okay?' she said with a smile but with sadness in her voice.

'I sure will Ruhi; you get home and get some sleep. Sorry for keeping you out till late.'

'Shut up! It was nice running into you, Adi,' she said cheerily before giving him a hug and a peck on his cheek. He felt the warmth of her body; he didn't want it to end this way. He wanted to see her again.

Aditya walked back to the hotel with thoughts of Ruheen and the things they had been through. He watched her walk away with the wind blowing through her long tresses. She looked even more beautiful than the last time they met, though in very different circumstances. She was a woman now, a strong independent woman. He ran into Mr Bakshi walking up to his room at the same time he walked in. The portly Sales Director had a smirk on his face.

'So *yaar*, how did your relaxing day go? It looks like you've been up to mischief yourself,' Bakshi said.

'It's nothing like that, Bakshi. I caught up with an old college friend. It seems like you've had a good day.'

'Yes, I sure have. Care to join me tomorrow ? I plan to visit a couple of erotic museums…'

'No you go ahead. I have some plans with this friend of mine. Goodnight,' Aditya said before heading down to his room at the end of the corridor.

7

The next day…

The next morning, Aditya got dressed lazily and was back at Fusion Café at 9 a.m.

'So we meet again,' she said with a bright smile and a twinkle in her eyes as she walked up to him with a mug of coffee.

'Yes, it would be tragic if we didn't,' he said.

'How did you sleep?' she asked with concern.

'Not much, I slept very little. What about you?' he asked with a grin.

'Not much either. Thanks to someone who messaged me through the night,' she said, feigning irritation.

'Yeah? So this guy is bothering you, huh? What's he like?'

'I'm sure you know him better than I do. You don't expect me to stand around and praise you…what do want for breakfast? The waffles with whipped cream are my favourite,' she said sweetly.

'Waffles with whipped cream it is. Ruheen, let's go away from here. Let's spend the day together, take a day off, I'm sure you can, right?'

'Adi…don't make it difficult for both of us. You don't want this, Adi! You don't deserve this trouble in your life. I'm married to this guy I've run away from. It's complicated and difficult, and I'm not sure I'm ready to get into a relationship.'

'Ruhi, it's me. I was a part of your life before any of this happened! I'm just saying, let's give it a shot. I've never met someone like you before and I've never loved a woman before the way I've loved you.'

'But then what happened, Adi? Vishal came and threatened

us, and everything between us went to hell.'

'I didn't intend it to end that way. I stayed away for a while because you asked me to. I felt I'd finish my exams and we could work things out. Before this happened you left…'

'I had to leave, Adi, for your safety and mine. Vishal had a guy watching both of us, all the time! His father was a big shot politician in Punjab. He was connected, and he was nuts! He was sending me MMS clips of you being followed. He asked me to leave the city before any harm came upon you. Vishal could do any damn thing he wanted. I left because I wanted both of us to live.'

'Anyway, that was in the past. What about today? What we have is now; we have our future ahead of us. I have a good job and a successful career, Ruheen,' he said in a persuasive voice.

'I don't want to have this conversation. Do you want anything else with your waffles?' she asked coldly.

'Another cup of coffee,' he said looking at her but she turned her gaze away and walked away.

She was back a few minutes later with his waffles and coffee. 'See, let's sit and talk about it. I'm going to wait for you at Dam Square. It's about the rest of our lives, Ruheen, let's spend some time before I leave, okay?'

'I won't be coming, Aditya, please don't wait for me. Enjoy the rest of the day. Say a little prayer for me when you can,' she said with tears in her eyes and walked away.

He waited at the Dam Square for her, thinking about the time they spent together the night before. He spent the entire day reading a book, waiting for her to come. He thought about the years gone by and felt that he should have done things differently. I should have confronted Vishal and called his bluff. *I should have gone down to Shimla soon after she did and persuaded her. She doesn't trust me any more. She feels I can't take care of her and protect her. Based on what happened in the past, she is right.*

He wallowed in memories of lost opportunities and self-loathing. *Why couldn't I have stood up for her and myself then? Why didn't I go to Shimla or to Delhi and look for her? For someone in love, I did very little but sit around and rue about Ruheen leaving Mumbai without telling me. For me, the exams or proving my worth in the management training phase were bigger priorities.*

By now afternoon turned into evening and evening was turning into night. At twilight, he caught a glimpse of her walking towards Dam Square.

'I heard 'With or Without You' three days back at the café near my place and remembered you and times we shared back in college. I remembered how you sang to me the other night, so many years ago. The next day you're here...right before my eyes, it's like a dream. So you did end up waiting all day?' she asked with a smile. She stood there with a glow on her face as she ran her fingers through her hair. She took off her large overcoat to reveal a figure-hugging black dress and sat down next to him.

'You bet, and I didn't think you would come. I began to lose hope...' he said with a relief.

'You lose hope very quickly,' she said with a smile. 'I came by a couple of times and watched you from a distance. I couldn't get myself to walk up to you. I was confused, I've been thinking all day...'

'Let's go and eat something, I'm hungry from all the waiting,' he said.

'Yes, you've been here for like eleven hours, you crazy man! Let's head over to Alfredo's around the corner. He makes great hand-tossed pizzas.'

'Maybe we can do a takeaway and head back to my hotel.'

'Maybe,' she said with a smile that would always haunt him. She put her arm in his as they walked to Alfredo's.

8

Two days later…

Aditya postponed his tickets by a couple of days, much to Ruheen's delight. Bakshi left that morning after giving him a sheepish grin. He knew that Aditya had company, and that something was going on.

'Ruhi, take off from work, that way we can spend some quality time together,' Aditya said, turning towards her, and running his fingers across her bare back.

'No,' she said firmly, turning around and looking at him with a deep frown.

'Come on, please! I have to go back to India in a couple of days.'

'Oh, of course, *baba*, you don't have to ask. I've already sent Desmond a text message,' she said, ruffling his hair with an impish grin before kissing him.

Aditya checked out from the hotel and they went back to her place. After a shower, they went down for breakfast at Klas, a nice brasserie for commuters at the Central Station.

They headed back to her place for a bit and then went out again. He asked Ruheen to take him around and show him some of the places he hadn't seen and which would be worth a visit.

They started with a trip to Oude Kirk, the oldest church in the city, built in the fourteenth century.

'I love the Renaissance façade above the northern portal,' Aditya said, looking up and admiring the structure. 'It does have some really interesting carvings.'

'This is also the place where Rembrandt's wife Saskia, who died in the seventeenth century, is buried,' Ruheen added.

'Yes, it's an interesting place with some shocking sights as well.'

They then took a tram to the Anne Frank Huis, the seventeenth-century canal-side house where the famous diarist and her family hid for two years during World War II. Ruheen snuggled closer to him and walked through the long line with her hand in his. They stopped to steal kisses while outside and were oblivious to the rest of the world around them.

An hour later, they walked over to Westerkerk, the old church and tower, which offered magnificent views.

'Apparently this is where Rembrandt and his son Titus are buried,' explained Ruheen while Aditya listened with interest and clicked away on his camera.

They managed to get to the top and see a splendid view of the city and its many canals.

'Beautiful, amazing!' Aditya exclaimed.

'Yes, it is, isn't it? I come here when I feel alone, it's a lovely view.'

'What view? I was talking about you,' he said with a grin.

She grabbed his camera and scrolled through the album to see pictures of her showing different expressions.

'You're nuts, Adi...' He had his arms around her waist and they kissed passionately, against a backdrop of canals, windmills and beautiful tulip fields extending into the far distance.

They moved on to a relaxed lunch at Envy, a nice Italian restaurant and Ruheen took him down to the American Book Centre, her favourite book store, and Blue Note from Ear & Eye, to pick some jazz and blues CDs that he had been searching for back in India.

Later that evening they went down to Kinetic Noord, a vibrant, cultural breeding ground for young artists and DJs. Aditya was fascinated by the place. He realized that Ruheen really knew her way around the city.

'Now I understand why you don't get bored. There's so much

to do out here,' he said eagerly.

'Well, not quite when you're alone. I'm having a better time today than I ever did on my own in this city,' she said, putting her head on his shoulders as the wind blew her hair into his face.

They went back to her apartment and made love. They couldn't get their hands off each other, and spent long moments locked in each other's embrace.

'Adi?'

'Hmm?'

'I can't believe this is happening...'

'This is?'

'Us, stupid! You and me, together, after like a zillion years,' she said, playfully biting his neck.

'When two people are meant to be together, the forces of nature conspire to bring them together,' he said, pinning her down and cuddling with her.

They went out to party later that night. Ruheen wore a cream skirt, one she had picked up and never worn before. She looked devastatingly beautiful with kohl lining her eyes and her soft brown hair falling over her shoulders. Neither of them had had a night out about town in a long time. They started with Strand West at The Jordaan itself, a nice place that played progressive house music and then moved across to Flexbar which played electro and hip-hop, where both of them partied till they were ready to drop dead.

Ruheen then cajoled him to check out one more place. 'Come on, Adi love, I haven't partied here till today. I don't want to be here with you, and not check out Jimmy Woo's. It's like the most popular haunt in town,' she said with her famous pout.

'Aah, that pout on your face and the look in your eyes that would make me kill if you asked me to. Let's go,' he said, 'Let's take a cab and head out there.' He walked out of Flexbar behind her and they headed for Jimmy Woo's, a popular new lounge.

'This is one of the most luxurious clubs I have seen,' Aditya said.

'It's the most happening of them all. See, it's packed with crowds even at 2 a.m., and the atmosphere is electric,' Ruheen preened.

The lounge was decorated with antique furniture and an uber-cool sound and light system. It was bustling with young party goers and the two of them danced till the club shut at 4 a.m., and walked out with their arms around each other.

Aditya's ears were still ringing from the loud music inside. Ruheen moved close to him with one hand ruffling his hair. 'I love you, Adi, you're the best thing that ever happened to me,' she said softly with a vulnerable look in her eyes, almost whispering in his ears.

He put his arms around her waist and told her what he felt about her while she gazed deep into his eyes with longing and passion. It was 5 a.m. by the time they got home. 'Let's get out of the city tomorrow. I know a couple of nice towns nearby,' she said as they walked up the stairs. Aditya couldn't take his eyes off her.

'Anywhere you want, Ruhi,' he said, following her into the apartment like a lost puppy. They fell asleep in each other's arms with no energy left to change.

■

The next morning they had an Arabic breakfast at Souq and left for Haarlem, the provincial capital, and a town built in the tenth century which was fifteen minutes away by train. Ruheen was quiet all the way and spent those minutes looking out of the window. Aditya figured that she was worried about him leaving the next morning. He could sense that she wanted him to stay on and be with her. She had taken an entire week off from the café.

To him she looked like an angel in her grey-black sweater and her figure-hugging blue jeans. They walked out of the station with her hand in his and visited the famous old church of St Bavo.

'This place houses the famous Muller organ, once played by Mozart when he was on a tour to the Netherlands as a young boy,' she said, as Aditya took it all in, more mesmerized by her presence.

They spent some time at the De Hallen and Teyler's Museum looking at works and drawings of current-day international artists and the Old Masters such as Rembrandt, Michelangelo and Raphael. They moved over to a quiet café by the canal at the main square, and after lunch, walked around the main square for a while. Ruheen dragged Aditya into some boutiques and bought him a couple of shirts; this seemed to cheer her up a little. He realized that she had seemed melancholy all day, and looked like she might burst into tears at any moment.

'Let's go and spend some time at Zandvoort Beach, it's just a cycle ride away from Haarlem,' she suggested.

The ride to the lovely beach brought some colour back into her face. They sat on the rocks watching the seagulls swoop into the water on sighting their prey and enjoyed the tranquil atmosphere, away from the hustle and bustle of the main square.

'So you really are going away, Adi,' she said, making a sad face looking away from him.

'Ruhi, I wish I never had to go back, but we've signed this really important deal. There's a lot of work piled up back home.'

'When can you come back?' she asked, turning her gaze and looking at him with searching eyes.

'Why don't you come back with me, Ruhi? I know you've been safe here, you have the café and everything...but I'll look after you, I'll make sure nothing happens to you. Let's go back, and work on building a future for ourselves.'

'Back in Mumbai again? I'm not so sure, Adi! I moved out of the city three years ago and I'm not sure if I want to go back. I don't have many pleasant memories, just those of the wasted years in college. Those years back when I was stupid and messed up,' she said in a low contemplative voice.

'It's also where we met and fell in love, Ruhi, if you remember.'

'I do, but we both know what happened after that. What if

Rohan lands up in Mumbai and tries to harass me? Besides what will I do out there, the city is too fast paced for my liking. I know you feel at home out there, I don't know about myself.'

'Maybe we can open a café for you. It's something you know you can do,' he said with a smile.

'Oh, I don't know, Adi, why don't we give it some time? On the one hand it will be very difficult to stay apart, but on the other hand moving to Mumbai right now...it seems a little rushed,' she said. He could sense the insecurity in her voice.

'Give it a shot, Ruhi, come and stay with me for a while. The winter is upon us in a few months anyway. Don't give up your apartment, come with me and we'll see how it goes. Let's give it our best shot to make it work, Ruhi,' he said persuasively.

She looked at him with searching eyes and then gazed into the distance. After about an hour she said, 'Okay, yes, Adi...let's do it. Let me call James and have a word with him. There's so much to do now! I need to get a ticket, we need to pack...'

He pulled her close and kissed her passionately. 'I already bought your ticket, sweetheart,' he said, waving a printout. 'We fly out of Amsterdam tomorrow morning at 7.15,' he said, beaming at her.

'What if I had said no to going back with you?' she asked.

'I wouldn't have gone either. I would have asked James to give me a job at the cafe,' he said with a sheepish smile.

'Right you would! That would have been a sight. Let's leave then, you scheming bad boy,' she said, tugging at his sweatshirt. 'I'll call James on the train; it's 5.30 already,' she said with excitement. The glow on her face and the happiness in her voice was something he saw for the first time in years. She seemed like the old Ruheen again, one who hadn't been through the nightmarish marriage and its aftermath.

They rode back to the main square, and took a train back to Amsterdam. From the station, they went to her café to say goodbye to her friends and colleagues who gave her an emotional send off. James and Shilpa called a couple of times asking her if she was sure of what she was doing. She assured them that she did, and that everything would be okay. They managed to make it back to her apartment and threw in some of the things she needed into a large suitcase. She didn't have much with her given that she had fled London with a small tote bag. The two of them went out and partied again at Badcuyp, a café lounge that played a mix of African music, jazz and salsa, just managing to make it back a couple of hours before they had to report at the airport.

That next morning, Ruheen and Aditya flew back to Mumbai to begin a new life together.

9

A week later...

Ruheen had moved into Aditya's apartment, a one-bedroom sea-facing apartment near Carter Road in Mumbai. She had just finished vacuuming the apartment, and plonked down on the couch. She felt extremely tired after cleaning the apartment and making space for her things for the past few days. She decided to go in for a shower as Aditya was expected home in an hour.

Coming back to Mumbai and staying with Aditya in his apartment was better than what she initially expected. She felt secure, especially given the nice place he stayed at and the lifestyle he could support. She remembered how high the cost of living was back then, when she was a student, over three years ago.

She spent some time going through the newspaper. She was looking for retail space to start a small French bakery as she had planned. She got out of the shower humming a tune a few minutes later, and added a new shower curtain on the list of things to buy. She heard the doorbell and opened the door to see Aditya with a bunch of lilies in his hand. She tugged on his tie and pulled him closer, giving him a kiss.

'How was your day?' she asked cheerfully.

'Same crap, no different from yesterday,' he said with a grin, running his fingers through her wet tresses. 'How was yours? What did you get up to?'

'Not too eventful, slept in till noon. I've been busy since. Do you notice anything different in the apartment?'

'No,' he said, looking around to spot something new. 'Except that the newspapers are nicely arranged.'

'Shut up! Adi, I've been cleaning since afternoon. Your *bai* is absolutely useless, a *kaam chor*! Can't you see the place is cleaner? I've changed the drapes, the sheets in the bedroom, cleaned the window panes, and the glass on the sliding door. Can't you see?'

'Ha ha, yes it looks a bit cleaner!'

'A bit?' she asked, feigning mock anger.

'It's spotless, love. It's sparkling clean, it's cleaner now, than when I first moved in,' he said with a straight face.

'You're making it up,' she said, turning around and heading to the kitchen. 'Will you have a cup of tea or coffee?'

'Anything you're having. What do you plan to do this evening ?'

'Hmmm, there's a long list of things we need. We could go shopping?'

'Like?'

'Like cutlery, an apron, gloves, a quilt, a toaster, maybe shower curtains, groceries…'

'Okay, I get the drift. Where do you want to eat tonight?'

'We'll eat at home. I've baked pasta, I hate going out to eat every day,' she said. He walked into the kitchen and put his arms around her while she waited for the water to boil.

'Let's eat at home and stay in. We can call for the groceries you need. I had some other ideas in mind about how we could spend the evening. We can shop for the other things you need over the weekend, what do you say?'

'Not a bad idea,' she said, putting her arms around his neck and kissing him again.

■

Ruheen spent a lot of time and effort in doing up the apartment. It was transformed from a bachelor pad into a cosy home in a few weeks. She bought paintings for the walls, organized the cupboards, bought new drapes, pots and plants in the balcony and set up the kitchen.

Aditya would come home every night, to be welcomed by a warm hug, and the aroma of delicious food on the table. On his way up, in the elevator, he could picture her opening the door for him with her apron on and a stunning smile. Sometimes she would surprise him by doing other things.

He had begun to leave work early in order to get home by 8 p.m. He also avoided travel, unless it was very necessary. Earlier, he would fly out almost every other week to manage campaigns in other cities or to study the market. He cut his trips down to once a month.

After she set the place up to her satisfaction, Ruheen decided to take it easy for a while. She wanted to take a break, and think about what she wanted to do. She caught up on books and movies. She spent hours watching some of TV series like *24* and *Prison Break* on DVDs, watching back-to-back episodes. Most of all, she felt at home, and felt loved after a long time.

On Saturday nights, Aditya often took her out to Squeeze or Red Light, which were her favourite haunts. Sometimes they went over to Zenzi near their place with a couple of friends. Most Sundays they would have breakfast at Just Around the Corner, where they spent the afternoon reading the newspaper or sipping coffee. In the evenings they would go out for a movie or a play depending on what was on, and often met Mohan and Vidya for dinner. Ruheen made an effort to get along despite the initial cold vibes she got from them. She played the perfect host and cooked a nice dinner for the two of them, finally managing to break the ice over a game of Scrabble.

Initially Mohan was very sceptical of Aditya's relationship with Ruheen, and was upset when Aditya first brought her back to Mumbai.

■

A month ago...

Mohan dropped into Aditya's office for a chat, after Aditya had called and told him whom he was living with. He sat back stone-faced while Aditya narrated what Ruheen had been through, and the time they spent together in Amsterdam.

'What are you doing boss? Are you nuts? You say she is married to some crazy guy, and here you are playing the hero and protecting her,' he said, removing his glasses and rubbing his eyes.

'I told you, dude, I have feelings for her. I'm in love with her, man; I don't care about any other guy! As far as she is concerned there is no one else in her life apart from me.'

'*Haan* hero, yes sure, you're her protector and saviour. You do remember what happened the last time, right?'

'Yes, we had trouble last time.'

'Why do you think so?'

'Because that guy was nuts. He went ballistic over the fact that I was dating his ex-girlfriend.'

'Because she is trouble, man, someone like her takes trouble with them wherever they go,' said Mohan.

'Relax, man, she's my girl, remember?'

'I do, but you better be clear in your head about what you're doing,' Mohan said firmly, not wishing to continue the debate.

'Yes, I will be. Besides, I'm not a college kid now. I have less to fear about people like these, this is my city now. I would love to see that moron of a husband come down and try anything funny. He won't have a leg to stand on.'

'Relax, Adi, I haven't seen you talk like this before. I'm just saying be careful. Last time something happened, she just packed her bags and fled the city, and you were miserable for months. Don't do something that will put you through misery. That's all I'm saying.'

'I know you mean well. Why don't the four of us go out for dinner this weekend? It will be nice for Ruheen to meet you guys. I don't want to get her too involved with the office bunch at this stage when we are just living together; they're a different sort. Besides, Ruheen doesn't really want to keep in touch with her old friends.

'Okay…we can do a coffee, we have a family thing lined up for Sunday but we could meet after that.'

'Let's do that,' Aditya said, walking him out. Then he headed off for a meeting.

∎

10

Four months later...

'Hi, can I call you back? I'm busy in a meeting,' Aditya said hurriedly.

'Adi, I'm at the auditorium already! How long will you take? The play starts in ten minutes. Don't tell me you're still in office,' Ruheen said with a hint of irritation.

'Oh damn, the play! I'm so sorry sweetheart. I've just been caught up fire-fighting all day. Please go ahead, don't wait for me. It's impossible for me to make it. I'll make it up to you. I'm sorry again.'

'Okay, fine, whatever. See you at home.' She hung up, and shook her head in dismay.

In the weeks that followed, Aditya found himself being stretched at work. He was working night and day to ensure that the launch of SK's Enigma brand of aftershaves and gels in India was a big success.

SK Products had grown to be the largest player in the hair oil and hair cream market during the licence quota raj. They were a case study in many B schools as Shudh and Shakti were iconic brands across markets in India which are diverse and have different forces at play with many regional players. But with liberalization and the entry of many global majors, the lustre of past successes in the Indian market began to fade. The big guys came in with big budgets for marketing and branding. They successfully segmented the market and targeted different niches, while SK Products was fighting to survive at the lower end of the market.

The company continued to do well in rural India, where people still watched their advertisements on Doordarshan and came to village *haats,* where they ran successful campaigns. Their well-established distribution channel helped greatly. But within urban India, they had become a spent force. Shakti and Shudh became products targeted at the lower income groups. Supermarkets and hypermarkets stocked very little of their products, just small quantities for the older generation who still believed in the products and asked for them.

SK Products' market share fell gradually over a period of ten years, to half of what it originally was. When Aditya joined the company, it was on a slide to the bottom and there was a considerable churn in the senior management over the years. Most of the star performers were lured with lucrative pay packages by the big boys. Those who stayed were old-timers like Bakshi who still reminisced about the company's golden years, and were adamant that SK Products was a great company doing a great job. The fact is they were afraid of change and were incapable of surviving in a competitive environment. The focus was more on defending and protecting their turf in rural India, while the competition chipped away at the company's bottomlines in big cities. The company had lost more than half their distributors in cities like Mumbai, Delhi, Bangalore and Hyderabad. Some of the distributors went bankrupt holding an inventory which didn't sell; while others moved on to take up the distribution of bigger and more successful brands.

For the company, licensing the Enigma range of products was like a second coming. Mr Kishore, the CEO, cleverly set up a separate team to work on this project launch, side-stepping any interference or control from the old guard. Aditya was called in to prepare a blueprint for the launch and present the sales and distribution strategy: first was the test-market of the products in Pune, then a big launch in Delhi, Mumbai, Chennai, Bangalore, Kolkata and Hyderabad, followed by a roll out in other cities over the next three months.

Anuj Suri, the Sales Manager who reported to Bakshi but

detested him was roped in to work with Aditya on sales and distribution and ensure that it was in sync with the marketing strategy. Nikhat Azmi, a whiz in finance, also a new joinee, was pulled in to handle budgets and manage the costing and pricing side of things.

The three of them worked like there was no tomorrow. Mr Kishore put in long hours himself and held long meetings with the team twice a week, running through their plans with a fine toothcomb and playing the devil's advocate. Aditya roped in interns from business schools and sent them into the field in different cities to see what the competition was doing. He carried out a complete time and motion study of the product, moving from the point of manufacturing to the point of sale. The team studied different models of distribution to try and figure out what would work best for them and what they could do better.

He took Ruheen along sometimes, and travelled to the metros to study campaigns that were afoot in different parts. He also became a mystery shopper for a few days and went to different stores asking about hair creams and hair gels, to figure out which products were being recommended to customers and why.

Mr Kishore, using his old boy network and his crafty selling skills managed to have the company strategically tie up with Healthy Foods India's distribution network across major cities. Healthy Foods focused entirely on the packaged foods market and had no intention of getting into personal care products. Enigma was launched with a big splash. They had Bollywood actor Rahil Khan with his hair gelled and styled differently every week, bare-chested with an air of supremacy staring out of hoardings and posters with 'Enigma Forever' splashed across his bare torso, and asking people on TV, 'Have you tried Enigma yet?' Next came a series of ads around the theme, 'An Enigma for every occasion', showing stills from Rahil Khan's movies, which showed him in different hairstyles and sporting different looks, beating up the bad guys, working out at the gym, riding a horse dressed as a gladiator, romancing a bombshell in the Swiss Alps, walking out of a meeting in a pin-stripe suit and sitting with his family for a meal in a restaurant.

They roped in Manisha Roy, his rumoured girlfriend, for an intimate shoot. Across cities, they had the two heartthrobs staring out of hoardings, Manisha Roy running her fingers through his hair and with a seductive smile saying, 'I love Enigma, do you?' and another with the couple in bed with Rahil Khan saying, 'I wonder what people find enigmatic about me?' before turning off the lights and the shot rolling over to the bathroom where it focuses on tubes of Enigma Wet Look styling gel and Enigma Strong Hold styling gel. The adverts were tongue-in-cheek and bold.

Mr Kishore was hesitant to take such an aggressive line but Aditya managed to convince him. Rahil Khan was the most loved and most enigmatic star of the current generation and had done very few campaigns at that time. His personality—brash, bold and living on the edge—was exactly the brand persona Aditya wanted for Enigma. He also pushed a few other innovative ideas by rolling out the Enigma Rahil Khan Collection, a premium range at upscale hair saloons across the metros. PR coverage of Rahil Khan walking into the saloon of his hairdresser friend and styling a customer's hair using Engima hair gel, was splashed across national dailies. The company managed to get premium shelf space across leading stores which were taken in by the buzz and the strong response to the initial marketing splurge. The plan of having Rahil Khan live the brand paid off, with the star writing about it on his blog, discussing it on his TV show and shown using it in his latest blockbuster.

Engima caught on and became a big success. SK Products followed up with the launch of aftershave gels, body sprays and lotions for men, all being a big success in aspiring India.

■

Aditya and Ruheen's relationship took a backseat during this phase;

Ruheen spent most of her time trying to find a suitable place in the neighbourhood to start her little bakery and café, but was unsuccessful. She encouraged Aditya through the stressful phase by standing by him and not making demands on his time. He would come back home late at night and talk to her about the sometimes unsuccessful meetings with the big stores, the advertising and media agencies he worked with and politics in office with the old guard who were doing all they could to create fear in the mind of Mr Kishore, telling him that he was being set up for disaster.

Six months after they had begun living together, he got back home one day in a terrible mood. It was past 11.30 p.m. and Ruheen was asleep. She got up and came into the living room, hearing the sound of the television.

'Hey Adi, how was your day? Should I make something for you? Have you eaten?' she asked, looking sleepy. She walked up and sat next to him on the sofa taking his hand in hers and looking at him with those dreamy eyes full of intensity and concern.

'You've had a rough day, I know. Do you have to go to Pune this weekend?'

'I don't know, Ruheen! I don't know how much longer I can go on like this. That damn Bakshi and his band of old clowns are trying to stall everything Anuj, Nikhat and I are trying to put together. They have some kind of hold over Mr Kishore, and keep scaring him about our plans. They tell him things like "Sir, if we do things like this we are finished" or "this is too big a risk to take sir, don't listen to people with little experience." I don't know what their intentions are!'

'Stop worrying so much, Adi. I believe in you. Just keep working sincerely as you do, and soon you'll be proved right. Mr Kishore is an intelligent man; there is a reason why he has you at the helm of affairs for Enigma and not Bakshi who has worked for him for over twenty years,' she said plainly with conviction in her eyes.

'You're right, but I get really tired fighting through all the politics within. It's not like everything outside is rosy. We have a long and tough battle to get through to make it a successful launch. Sometimes, I want to quit and take up...' he said feeling distraught.

'Take it easy, Adi, I don't want you to give up. I want you fight through this and succeed, I'm with you on this,' she said, running her fingers through his hair and kissing him softly.

After a few moments of silence, cupping his cheeks in her hands she said, 'Let's go away for the weekend, you need a break. You've worked for over four weeks without a day off. You can't live like this Adi.'

'I have planned a visit to the key stores in Kolkata this weekend,' he said with a tired smile and added, 'you know what, screw it. I'll go on Monday, let's take a break. You need a break too. Where do you want to go?'

She looked at him with a sweet smile and kissed him again. 'Let's go to Goa, I love the beaches...'

'How about Juhu Beach?'

'Ha ha really, we can eat bhelpuri and ride on that poor camel. It sure will be one pleasant weekend,' she said with mock sarcasm and frowned at him.

'I'm kidding, love, let me book the flights tomorrow morning and the Hyatt for the weekend. We'll leave on Friday afternoon and aim to get back early on Monday morning.'

'Sounds like a plan,' she gushed, wrapping her arms around him. Moments later he carried her into the bedroom—she had fallen asleep in his arms.

A week later...

Aditya and Ruheen flew down to Goa the following weekend and had a blissful time, just enjoying being with each other. They swam in the sea, went parasailing and took long walks on the beach. Ruheen clicked away pictures of them together. She was in better spirits since she had got out of the routine of sitting at home and waiting for something to happen.

While they lay down in their cottage after a swim, she said, 'It's been a wonderful break, Adi, it was really nice to get away and come down here.' She seemed to be happier than he had ever seen her—the scars from the past seemed like a distant memory.

'It sure has, Ruhi,' he said, putting his arm around her. 'Thanks for convincing me to take a break. I really needed to recharge my batteries and get set for a long battle against the odds till the launch.'

'Hmm...you've got to take it easy after the launch, Adi. It isn't good for you to keep working like this, it's stressful for you... stressful for us,' she said softly, sounding concerned.

'I will slow down, I'm sorry. The past few months have been unbelievably crazy. I feel terrible and guilty as we haven't spent much time together; in fact we haven't even stepped out for a meal or a coffee in the last couple of months.'

'I know, but it's okay. I want you to be successful at what you do! If it means a little bit of sacrifice now, I'm okay with it,' she said with warmth.

'But we should get away like this more often. Take some short trips, where I can just spend time with you and not have to bother about Enigma or anything else.'

'It's all right, I've been busy myself, trying to figure out what to do and get started with something. I've seen that rents are very high in our neighbourhood and some others. It's too expensive to start something here. Rents are at over a lakh a month for a matchbox. It's beyond me to work with such overheads, besides there are so many cafés around...'

'So what do you have in mind?' he asked.

'Rita Doshi who owns Flavours, is willing to put a counter in the restaurant and let me run it on a fifty-fifty partnership basis. I supply the cakes and she takes care of everything else. This sounds better, though I would rather supply the pastries at a certain agreed rate and she could sell them at any price she wants. I'm discussing these things out with her. She says that she can also get me orders from offices and homes for birthdays and other special occasions. This itself should keep me going,' she said proudly.

'I'm proud of you, Ruhi!' he said, elated by what she had managed to pull together. 'Let's think of ways to better market your range of pastries. After all you've been well trained by Henry back in Amsterdam.'

'I know, what do you suggest, Mr Brand Manager?'

'I was thinking let's call this 'Sinful Seductions by Ruheen Oberoi'—I could arrange to have you talk about it in a couple of newspapers. With a face like yours, they'll be more than happy to get a picture in. Besides, we could do a simple website or a blog where you could put up pictures of pastries, talk about making them. Maybe, we could also have handouts given out at Flavours and a few supermarkets. I could arrange all of this, don't worry.'

'Like I said, when we first met, you're a super intelligent dude. I don't know where you come up with such ideas.'

'I don't know how you manage to look heavenly every single day.'

'Flattery, huh?' she said, playful pushing his arm away from her knee. 'On most days, you ignore your so-called heavenly creature that inhabits the same space as you.'

'I know, I'm wasted at the end of the day. What can I do now to make up for it?' he asked with genuine interest.

'Let's go to Amsterdam in September, it will be nice to go back there. It'll be about a year since we got back together, by then,' she said and got up to walk down towards the beach.

'Sure, let's go, I can't wait to put on my party hat. Let me apply for leave as soon as the campaign finishes.'

'Wonderful, can we do one more thing?'

'This is likely to be around the time of my birthday, can we spend it in Paris? I lived there for over a year, and still didn't manage to visit Paris. Please Adi, I really want to go!' she said with her pout and the wind in her hair.

Despite living together for a year, Aditya couldn't get enough of her. He was still so smitten, still so drawn to her, like a moth to a flame.

'We can go to the moon if you would like to! Sure, let's go to Paris, anywhere your heart pleases,' he said before she shut him up by drawing his lips into hers.

Sitting on the towel and watching the sun go down, he gazed at her intently, staring far out into the emptiness of the sea where time stood still. 'Ruheen, can I ask you something?'

'Yes, anything Adi; tell me, what is it that you want to ask me?' she asked.

He didn't want her to misread his intentions. He couldn't ask her to marry him; if he could he would.

'I was wondering if you missed your grandpa and if you wanted to go and pay him a visit...'

'I don't know if it's the best thing to do, Adi. I'm not sure if he ever forgave me; I made some horrible choices and put him through a lot of misery. I have called him a few times over the years but he speaks to me for a minute, answers the usual questions about his health and hangs up. I don't think I have the guts to go down there, Adi,' she said with moist eyes.

'I'll come with you; I will be spending most of next month in Delhi and Chandigarh, studying the market and planning for the launch. You can fly in with me to Chandigarh, and we could drive down there on a weekend.'

'Are you sure that you want to do this?' she asked with tears running down her cheeks.

He wiped her cheeks and drew her close, 'Apart from me, he's all you have. Let's go and pay him a visit. Don't worry, I won't let him bite you.'

'He can't, he has no teeth! He lives on a diet of rice, dal, banana and yoghurt,' she said with a laugh.

'I prefer Ruheen in my diet,' he said with a smirk, sipping on his pint of beer.

'I'm sure you do, big boy, let's head back, and start packing. The sun has set on our weekend in Goa,' she said with a glitter in her eyes, as they walked back hand in hand on the wooden pathway towards the cottage.

■

They rented a car in Chandigarh, and drove down to Shimla a few weeks later. Ruheen looked nervous and jittery through the drive, while Aditya took the beauty of the queen of hills as they climbed higher and higher towards their destination. Ruheen's Nana, retired Major General Sumant Oberoi lived on a sprawling estate, a few kilometres away from the town, in a place called Mashobra. They had to take a number of diversions to get to the place as the bypass through some parts of the town was not an option, given the recent landslides.

They walked into the palatial bungalow, surrounded by lush green pine and cedar, four hours after starting out from Chandigarh. The servants at the gate gave Ruheen a big smile and welcomed them in. Ruheen stood behind Aditya as he walked up to greet the stocky old man with a walrus moustache, dressed in an oversized sweater. He had gentle eyes which radiated warmth. Aditya noticed where Ruheen got her eyes from; to Aditya, he certainly seemed like an amiable personality.

'You came after all these years to see me, my little one?' he asked gently, rising up from his armchair.

'I'm sorry, Nana,' she said, running towards him while he wrapped his big arms around her. Both of them cried for a while before they sat down together for a cup of tea.

'So you are the young man who took my child away to London?' he asked with a piercing gaze while lighting his pipe. Aditya decided not to reply, with Ruheen was away using the restroom.

The bungalow and the old Major General seemed straight out of a 1960s Hindi film. There were portraits on the walls, pictures of ancestors and those of the family in good times. It was clear that the good times had passed and things were falling apart. It seemed like the house had not been painted for years. 'When do the two of you plan to start a family?' he asked meekly as he saw Ruheen walk into the room.

Ruheen and Aditya looked at each other with surprise. Aditya gathered that he knew very little about what her life had been for the past two and half years. Aditya sat back admiring the chandelier above his head, and the portraits that adorned the walls, while Ruheen reluctantly began. She explained what had happened leaving out the more gruesome details of forced intercourse and physical abuse. Nana seemed upset hearing all this and Ruheen sat by his feet with her head on his knee, as he ran his palm over her head. He seemed to like Aditya and asked him to play a game of chess with him after tea.

The next day, Aditya went back to Chandigarh to wind up some unfinished work, while Ruheen decided to stay with Nana for a week and repair the broken bonds. Nana was keen on Ruheen filing for a divorce and said that he could have people he knew to take care of it, as the marriage was held in India. Aditya decided to stay out of it and let Ruheen handle things with him.

Nana walked with him to the gate, making Aditya promise to come again in a few months. He thanked him profusely for taking care of Ruheen, and bringing her back to India. 'She's the best thing that's happened to my life,' Aditya said, meeting his gaze and shaking his hand, while his eyes glowed with pride. Aditya noticed that he wasn't used to hearing praise being heaped on Ruheen.

Ruheen stayed behind for a minute, after her Nana walked back. She had feelings for Aditya in her eyes, those that he had never seen, some form of new-found respect. 'Thanks Adi, this is the best thing I've done in a long time. Thanks, for making me do this,' she said before burying her face into his chest, while he wrapped his arms around her.

12

Six months later...

They had had a good few months together with 'Sinful Seductions by Ruheen Oberoi' becoming the toast of the season back in Mumbai. Ruheen began to supply cakes and pastries to the crème de la crème of Mumbai. She also added on staff, and trained them diligently to cope with the demand for cakes and pastries. She was supplying to weddings, film premieres, anniversaries and birthdays all over the city. Many people wanted to franchise her brand to cities like Delhi and Bangalore, cities the opportunists liked to describe as 'high potential' markets. She had reluctantly come on the holiday to Amsterdam and Paris, leaving business in the hands of her now well-trained staff, after much cajoling by Aditya, who spent considerable efforts planning the holiday.

He needed a long break as well, as he had had a busy year at work, with the launch of Enigma and the success that followed. The competitors tried to take SK Products out of the reckoning by inking strategic deals for product placement within leading stores, and lowering prices to tempt them to get into a price war. Aditya's strategy to hold back on SK's higher prices and go on an offensive with an advertising campaign paid off rich dividends. Rahil Khan did a series of campaigns talking about cheap things he didn't buy, especially cheap hair products. 'Your hair says a lot about your personality, boss!' was his punch line. It worked to their advantage, and the low prices made the big boys bleed for six months, before better sense prevailed. Once they increased their prices to match Enigma's price, the little market share that they had gained, selling products below cost was also lost. Aditya was named the 'Brand Manager of the Year 2006' by *Marketing Jungle* magazine.

Mr Kishore kept talking about retirement and even dropped hints to friends in the media that in a few years, Aditya would be in the running for his job. Mr Kishore had now put Anuj, Nikhat and Aditya—who were riding high on Enigma's success—on the job of reinventing the Shudh and Shakti brands, and positioning them as brands for urban India. All in all, things were looking up for the both of them. They had both tasted success and had promising careers ahead.

Following the success back home, Ruheen and Aditya were on a much deserved break in Paris. The past six months had just flown by, and apart from the weekend with Nana in Shimla, they had spent very little time together; and this too, was spent making appearances at dos for their business associates. Being young, they had decided to network as much as possible as it certainly helped Ruheen's business as well as Aditya's career as a young business executive.

It was Ruheen's twenty-fifth birthday. She brought in her birthday on the balcony of their hotel room with a dark chocolate cake and a bottle of champagne. Aditya took her shopping in the morning after breakfast at Paul, and then to the Eiffel Tower, where they spent a few hours till sunset, followed by dinner at Moulin Rouge. They got back after a long night at the Moulin Rouge to their rooms at the Ritz Carlton. They didn't have much to drink but Ruheen was a little tipsy. She looked stunning that night in a grey-black outfit and her hair let loose just the way he liked it. He gave her a diamond bracelet and earrings on her birthday with a note that said, '*To my ravishing beauty, stay the beautiful person you are. Happy birthday, with love—Adi*'.

'How long did it take you to come up with this, Adi?' she asked with grin, trying on the earrings back in their room.

'Not long,' he said, walking up to her and putting his arm around her neck.

'I want to know like how long, tell me?'

'An hour, maybe two,' he smiled sheepishly.

'I knew it! You aren't too good with writing mushy notes, are you? But you are good at shopping for a woman. Thanks, I love them,' she gushed.

'That's not all, open your bag, there's a little more.' She walked up to her bag, opening it with curiosity while setting her gaze on his. She pulled out a red Calvin Klein bag and removed the gift-wrapping paper.

'You didn't,' she said, unravelling her little gift. 'I can't believe you actually walked into a store and bought this!'

'Yes I did. Now you might want to do me a favour and put it on.'

'Five minutes,' she said with a self-conscious smile, before walking towards the restroom.

'Ruhi, I'm not putting it on tonight,' he said before kissing her on the nape of her neck, as she slid into bed next to him.

'I don't have pills with me Adi, what do you mean?' She looked confused and rolled over to the other side of their king-size bed.

'Do you remember what Nanaji asked us six months ago? He wanted to know when we planned to start a family,' he said with a smirk.

'He did, but to start with he thought you were someone else,' she said, taking out her pack of cigarettes and lighting up. She looked confused and worried.

'But what's stopping us? We are in love and we have a stable future. Your divorce should be through in a few months as well. I want to start a family with you, Ruhi,' he said, rolling over to her side, and rubbing her bare thigh.

'Adi,' she said. She turned her gaze to meet his, 'Isn't it a bit too early? I've just started out; maybe we can wait for a bit. Let's not rush into something like making babies, this is huge!'

'Ruhi,' he said with conviction, 'trust me, we'll be fine. The baby will bring us closer together! In fact, I'm thinking of quitting in a couple of years, and becoming a freelance marketing consultant to companies. I intend to spend time and raise my kids…our kids. Imagine our own little ones, who will have your cute chin, your sweet smile and maybe your doe eyes.'

'Adi, stop it!' she said playfully, getting on top of him. 'This isn't marketing ice cream to Eskimos, mister! It's about bringing little lives into this world. Are we ready for it?' she asked while he nodded in the affirmative. She hesitated first, and smiled back at him before they slowly began to undress each other.

They made love that night, first with frenzy and then again slowly and passionately. As they had imagined, by the time they got back Ruheen was pregnant with their first baby.

13

A few weeks later...

Ruheen and Aditya got back from the trip to Amsterdam and Paris in good spirits. After a few days in Paris, they spent over a month in Amsterdam living in Ruheen's apartment. Both of them had a relaxed holiday; they slept in till late every day and took short trips all over the country. They also ended up partying like there was no tomorrow. It was there that they got to know about Ruheen's pregnancy. She did a test a couple of days before they left for India, and sure enough, her first baby was on its way. Both of them were elated, though a tad nervous about what lay before them, and came back happier and truly rejuvenated.

Mohan and Vidya walked into Aditya's apartment with a bottle of wine. Both of them embraced him, elated with the news of Ruheen's pregnancy.

'Look who is all set to be a daddy,' Vidya said with a grin.

'You're a real star, man! You've got promoted this year, and to add to it you'll be a father soon,' Mohan said, as Vidya walked into the kitchen to greet Ruheen who was supervising the maid.

'Thanks, man, I'm glad both of you could make it for dinner.'

'How could we not make it? This is huge, how's Ruheen doing?' Mohan asked.

'She's okay, she's very nervous about the whole thing. I've been buying a lot of books for her to consult.'

'I can imagine, Vidya was no different when she first got pregnant. Let me go and say hi to her.'

He was back in a few minutes, and joined Aditya in the balcony.

'So, how does it feel? Are you sure about this, given her divorce is yet to come through?'

'I haven't been more certain about anything in my life. I really want to do this. I want to start a family with Ruheen and raise our kids. It's what I look forward to, it'll be my legacy,' he said, with the sea breeze in his hair.

'Kids? Hold it there, brother. Do you know how much trouble they are? They can be quite a handful. We hardly get time together since we had Aarav; they need all your time and attention.'

'I'm ready for it, man, I want to be a hands-on father. I want to teach them how to ride a bicycle, take them swimming or teach them maths. I want to be a better dad than my father was. He was aloof and distant; he spent most of his waking hours at work or reading the newspaper while at home. I didn't know who he was really, just someone I respected and feared. I don't want to be someone who pays the bills and puts food on the table.'

'I know you want to be involved, most of us do. But remember the work stress we have to deal with. I can hardly spend time with Aarav, I'm working most weekends.'

'Hmmm…' Aditya gazed out into the distance, watching the tide come in, and a huge wave crash against the rocks at the seaface.

■

'It was quite a pleasant surprise when you called last week from Amsterdam. I had no clue you and Adi were trying for a baby,' Vidya said.

'We weren't, it just happened. Aditya said let's take the plunge and start a family…' a pale-looking Ruheen said, before drawing up a chair and sitting down at the small table in the kitchen.

'Are you ready for this then?'

'I'm not sure.' Ruheen sat back and closed her eyes for a moment. 'I saw the look in Adi's eyes when he said he wants to do this. He's ready, I feel. I guess I'm okay, I'm happy. Actually I don't know, I'm a bit nervous. I chatted with my Nana for hours;

I'm so anxious yeah, I don't know anything about raising a kid…'

'Well none of us do, it comes naturally once the baby arrives. But I get what you mean, I had similar fears. This is why I had my mum over for three months and didn't let her out of my sight.'

'Lucky you, I don't believe I have that luxury,' Ruheen said, with a deep frown.

'Don't worry, I'm here right? Everything will be okay; you have Adi by your side as well.' Vidya placed her palm on hers.

'Ha ha yes, he's been buying books on parenting like crazy,' she said. 'Let's call the guys, dinner is ready.'

■

'You were the perfect host tonight, you must be very tired,' Aditya said, while getting into bed next to Ruheen.

'God, I'm so tired! And I'm going to wake up wanting to throw up. Why do we have to do all the hard work?'

'I'll hold your hair back while you throw up,' Aditya said with a laugh. Ruheen picked up a cushion and swung it at him playfully.

'Yes, I remember that party at Red Light many years ago,' she said.

'Also, the time you threw up after we partied in Amsterdam, last year, my love.'

'Well okay, I get it.'

'And last month, Amsterdam again.'

'Shut up!' she said, moving closer towards him. 'Adi?'

'Yeah.'

'What do you think our children will be like?'

'Hmm…let's see. If it's a boy, he'll be all chubby and cute. You're going to end up spoiling him rotten with your pampering.'

'Is that right?' She sat up with a smile.

'Yes, though I'll make sure he plays a lot of sports. I'll make him swim and take him for tennis.'

'Ha ha, he might end up becoming a bookworm like you.'

'I hope not! I hope he joins the army or becomes a pilot. I'd be more proud if he did that than become some banker on Wall Street or a lawyer from Yale.'

'Is it? What if it's a girl?'

'Then I'll have trouble, because she's likely to be as beautiful as you are. I'll be quite protective, though I hope she grows up to become an artist of some sort. She could become a writer or a musician or maybe even an actor.'

'You really think about all this, don't you?' she said, ruffling his hair.

'Kind of, yeah. I want to raise this family of a bunch of free-spirited kids—writers, artists, musicians, pilots, even activists. I don't want them to do things for money, want them to be passionate, to believe in something. I'll make sure there's enough to let them do what they want.'

'Why not become a chef or a school teacher?'

'I don't mind, why not? We'll have one of each.'

'Sssh! What do you mean one of each? I'm no baby-making machine. What did you want to be while growing up?'

'I don't know, maybe a doctor when I was a kid. But I haven't thought about it for a long time. I guess I've gone with what works best for my career, and what can help me earn a good pay package. I probably am good at what I do, but I don't love it.'

'You're very good at what you do,' she said, leaning in and kissing him on his cheek. 'I'm scared, Adi.'

'Don't be, I'm with you. We'll be okay, all right?' he said, as his gaze locked with hers.

'Yes,' she said softly, before lying down.

14

A few days after their return, Aditya got a call from Ruheen who was sobbing at the other end.

'What happened, Ruheen? Are you all right?' he asked worriedly.

'Are you busy? When can you get home?'

'*Kya hua?*' he asked, puzzled by her outburst. She had been in low spirits over the past week, given her morning sickness. He picked up his keys and walked towards the elevator. 'Okay, I'm coming home,' he said.

Ruheen rushed into his arms when he got back. She looked pale and upset.

'I got back to work this morning to discover that I have been shafted by the owners of Flavours. They have removed my name and carried on business in the name of Sinful Seductions, with the staff that I had invested in and spent months training,' she said with tears running down her cheek.

'What? I haven't asked you this before, but you've agreed to something in writing with them, right?' Aditya asked in surprise.

'No, they said let's just split whatever we make, we are friends, why get into formalities.'

'How could they? Bloody hell, we don't have anything in writing. What about your staff?'

'Damn, I told you, Adi, they've taken on my staff as their own. They know what to do and how to do it. She has the retail front end and is obviously paying them more.'

'That snake, did you speak to her?'

'I did, the bitch said, "I'm sorry sweetie, I didn't think you would come back." She says she'll pass on some party orders to me,' Ruheen said, looking cross with herself.

'Ruheen, Ruheen, how could we be so naïve? This is such a dog-eat-dog world. You can't trust anyone here,' he said.

'Thanks, that makes me feel better, Adi. Can't you be a little more supportive?'

'What do you want me to say? Anyway, what's done is done. You take it easy, we'll figure something out. It isn't good for you or the baby if you take on this kind of stress. I'm sorry, but we'll work something out. Everything happens for the best,' he said, tucking her in bed and putting a pillow under her head.

Aditya was irritated with her and himself. They had trusted these people blindly and they took her for a ride. He kept kicking himself for not making an agreement, and setting this up formally as a company. Ruheen was not inclined to focus on these aspects, while he was busy managing a stressful career. Ruheen put on a brave face and lay low for a while. She was still basking in the glow of her pregnancy and decided not to get into a full-blown confrontation with the folks at Flavours. A few weeks later, she set up 'Selections by Ruheen Oberoi', and she worked on supplying a premium range to Banyan Tree Café, a quaint little place run by a nicer bunch of people, as well as taking on orders for birthdays and the like. But it was challenging and frustrating for her to do everything from scratch, aside from having rivals from Flavours snapping at her heels and lowering prices to undercut her. They got hold of her price list and offered their selection at 20 per cent lower than the price she quoted for party orders. They also offered thirty-day payment terms and discounts on future orders which she found unsustainable.

'Hi, this is Ruheen,' she said, picking up the phone one morning.

'Ms Oberoi, sorry we need to cancel our order for pastries with you. Flavours Café is doing the catering and they are offering us a food and dessert combo at a cheaper price,' the party planner for the upcoming celebrity wedding said.

'We could discuss the price if you would like…'

'No thanks, Ms Oberoi. We have already placed our order with them.'

Initially, Ruheen tried to fight it out by aggressively trying to market her Selections to past customers.

'Mrs Bhatt, this is Ruheen. Do you remember me? We did the cake for your daughter's birthday and your anniversary.'

'You're from Flavours right?' the voice at the other end said.

'No, Mrs Bhatt, you see I've branched out on my own, we are called Selections by Ruheen Oberoi.'

'Oh.'

'Maybe I can supply your requirements directly this year. I could do it at a cheaper rate as well…'

'We've already decided on doing my daughter's party at Flavours Café, dear. On our anniversary we are going away. But if this is your number, I'll let you know if ever I need something.'

'Thanks, Mrs Bhatt,' she said, before hanging up and walking out to the balcony with her cup of tea. All the hard work she had put in to establish her brand and build her reputation had gone to waste. She wondered whether she had the energy to start all over again, especially with the baby on the way.

■

A week later…

At Aditya's end, the situation changed drastically at work. Two weeks after they got back, he was called into Mr Kishore's office.

'Aditya! Come in, take a seat. So how is Ruheen, and how was Amsterdam? I've been in Delhi the last couple of weeks,' he said cheerfully while tapping on his desk.

'We had a wonderful trip, thanks. Ruheen's in the family way, so it's been good. A lot of changes at our end, things are happening quickly,' Aditya said with a quiet smile.

'Ah, exciting news, that's wonderful! Both of you must come home for dinner next week.'

'Sure, we'll work it out. With her morning sickness and the things she's going through, she has to be in a mood for it. Tell me, what's been happening here? Things seem quiet back in the office.'

'This is between us and a couple of others,' he said, looking at Aditya with a familiar smile, and added wisely, 'I've decided to sell the company to Healthy Foods India. I'm old and tired. This company has been my life, but I have to move on. I don't want to die selling hair oil.' He sat back with a smug grin, while Aditya was stunned, having failed to see that anything like this was coming.

'Their offer was good, Aditya; it was in fact very flattering, indeed. We can only go this far; it's tough to be independent and survive in this market. The global majors have ambitious plans; anyway Healthy Foods, which will change their name to Indiana Products, has a good long term strategy. Acquiring us gives them a strong position in the personal care products space. We have dominant brands here, and their aim is to also get into soaps, shampoos and oral care products. The family will manage the group company, while foods and personal care products will be run as separate business divisions. They want you on as VP, Marketing, for the whole company. They've asked me to discuss this with you—one reason they're paying me so much is to take people like Anuj and you on board. We're letting old-timers like Bakshi take an early retirement. I've spoken to him already and he leaves at the end of the week.'

Aditya sat back listening to him lay out plans that were in action, and the decisions that had been taken. He had a lot of respect for this affable old man, and knew he had the best intentions for his favoured employees.

'What do you suggest I do? Stepping into this role will take a lot of re-orienting and adapting, as the rules of the game change.

I'm not so sure. I feel there will be a clash between the divisions and roles like marketing. The question is who owns the brand, and who takes the decisions,' Aditya said with scepticism, wondering why he wasn't picked to lead one of the business divisions.

'The Chairman's younger son and his daughter will be the heads of the foods and personal care products division respectively, while the older one, Raman, who currently runs Healthy Foods will be the Group CEO. Your role will mainly be to support them and give advice…'

'So a powerful role in theory then…'Aditya said tersely.

'You could say that, but it's a step up the ladder for your career to oversee such a large portfolio at your age. Take this job; it will help your career in the long run. I know that they aim to take you on at a much higher package, while for some others they will be offering existing or lower packages,' he said assertively. *Clearly, he had been asked to sell the job and make sure I stay*, Aditya thought. *It must have been a part of the deal, and Mr Kishore sure was a good businessman.*

'Let me think about it, give me a couple of days. I could always sell my shares in the company and leave,' Aditya said, putting him on the back foot.

'Yes, you could,' he said, almost jumping out of his chair, 'I hope you realize that you're half my age, you have a whole lot ahead of you. You have a baby along the way; you can get a little more adventurous in life later on.'

'So who is the Chairman's daughter?' Aditya asked trying to change the topic.

'Sakshi Agarwal, she's twenty seven. An MBA from Columbia, and has worked for Wall Street Consulting in Chicago for a couple of years before coming back to Mumbai.'

'Marvellous, we have exciting times ahead don't we?' he said with sarcasm. 'When do you announce this to the world? When do you leave in this case?'

'We have a press conference tomorrow morning at the Taj Bayview—you need to be there. We need to meet the people on their side for dinner tonight. I leave at the end of the week; I will, however, come back after a few months to play an advisory role. There's only so much of golf you can play in a day.'

'You can't let go, can you? What happens to Anuj?' Aditya asked with a grin while relaxing a bit. He thought, *maybe being a part of Indiana Products was the best thing for the company.*

'He'll report to Shikha, he will be the General Manager of Sales for the personal care products business division. A move up the ladder for your good friend as well,' he said, walking Aditya out of his office.

■

The next evening, Aditya and Anuj drove down for drinks at Hard Rock Café, to discuss the options they had before them.

'So you've decided to take it, huh?' Aditya asked Anuj.

'Yes, *yaar*, I've kind of grown used to the company and our way of working. Changing jobs now will be an ordeal. I've only just got married,' he said, sipping on his beer.

'That's right, I'm still in two minds. I'm convinced that this whole merger isn't going to work, at least not with the proposed new boss's kids at the helm. It's going to become a circus, I don't think I will enjoy doing what I do under the new leadership,' Aditya said with conviction.

'We've built Enigma, man.'

'Right, but we aren't indispensable. Nobody is,' Aditya said.

'What makes you want to stay then?'

'It's the sense of security in this job. What I'd really like to do is probably travel a bit, open a small freelance consulting firm of my own and possibly teach. But there isn't security at the end of this. I've been through a tough phase during my teens. Post-liberalization, my dad lost his contract to supply components to the government watch company. It became a sick unit, all that he was owed was written off. We soon lost a lot of what we had back then, we learnt to make do with less. He tried his hand at other businesses but with limited success, till the illness took him. This is why I had to scrape through what remained, and work after college while I did my graduation to save up for an MBA. It wasn't easy pulling through—maybe if I had the means I could have gone to an Ivy League school. I had a 50 per cent scholarship for an MBA at Duke, but the bank was unwilling to lend Rs 10 lakh without collateral. Ruheen and I are having a baby; I want to give them the best, man. I want to take care of them, and provide for them. I don't want them to worry about anything.'

'But surely you have other options,' Anuj said.

'Yes, but like you said, change isn't easy. I do have an option in Singapore and one in Chennai, but I don't feel convinced about uprooting Ruheen again and putting her through this. She's been through a number of problems; even now with her business it is tough. I don't mind putting up with some crap at work myself. I want to insulate her and our baby from all this.'

'At some level it will affect both of you. Your role will be especially tough, given that you'll have to work with all the business divisions, but let's hope we survive.'

'Amen to that man, cheers!' Aditya said. *Yes, I hope everything will be okay.*

15

10 weeks later...

The next few months at work, as Aditya rightly predicted, were horrendous; the company had a structure only in name. The brothers and sister ran the company and their respective fiefdoms as they pleased. Matters got political, firstly with the folks back at Healthy Foods trying to show who the bosses were, and who had been bought over. Soon there were camps and cliques. Each of the scions was heralded in the business press as the young business icons of the new millennium. There was an unchecked appetite for extending the portfolio, and expanding the business with little or no market or feasibility studies.

The food products division with the Healthy Foods brand forayed into chips, biscuits, juices and chocolates from cooking oil, wheat flour and packaged tea, coffee and *masalas*. The personal care products division went further and launched Ria, a range of cosmetic products for women, Fresh toothpaste, diaper pads and a range of premium fragrances for men and women. Instead of growing stronger and launching product variants to address market niches, the organization was spreading itself thin and growing like there was no tomorrow.

People were recruited from different competitors at unheard of salaries, and they bought their band of followers with them. Shikha often led strategy workshops and brainstorming sessions, where only she spoke and everyone agreed with what she said. There was a use of consulting buzzwords and marketing jargon, but very little in terms of substance.

People like Anuj and Aditya saw a company they helped

transform retreating into the Middle Ages. Everything revolved around power and influence. Those who had access to the boss, called the shots, even if they were management interns or administrative assistants. Agencies were angry with the way in which the company worked on campaigns and kept changing things to please the new bosses, while distributors were fuming about the constant changes in promotions, pricing and sales offers.

Aditya got back home irate and frustrated every other day, given that he often had to do things that he was told to do, whether it was something he agreed with or not. This took a toll on Ruheen and their relationship. She increasingly began to feel unloved and unappreciated, while Aditya came across as being moody and irritated all the time. They had a few nasty rows, when she broke down and sobbed, and they didn't speak for a couple of days. They would make up after a while and laugh about it, but life was difficult. Both of them were on the edge, she with the pregnancy and he with a completely changed atmosphere at work. Aditya did try to be more patient and tried being there for her; it didn't help that they only had each other to vent their frustrations upon. Neither of them had family around who could absorb some of the pressure, and the responsibilities. Friends, much like them, were busy going through the motions with work, family and life.

One day, Aditya returned home late after a heated exchange with Shikha, on the proposal to launch women's deodorants under the Enigma brand.

'You're finally home; you could have messaged that you'll be late,' Ruheen said. She was in a surly mood waiting up for him.

'Sorry, I got held up in meetings. I should have called you,' he said in a tired voice.

'It's okay, come and sit. Let's eat, I made *paratha*s today. The cook didn't come, I decided to make something myself,' she said, while laying the table.

'Actually, you didn't have to. I'm not really hungry; I ate a couple of slices of pizza in the evening.'

'Adi, come on, just sit down and eat!'

'Stop being a baby, Ruheen. I don't know why you put yourself through this and cook. I'm not hungry and I don't want to eat.'

'Aditya, I've put in so much of effort, just sit down and eat them. Is there any appreciation for the effort I've put in, despite my condition?' she said raising her voice.

'Ruheen, babe, I don't want to eat the damn *paratha*s. I'm really tired; I'm not in a mood…'

Tears rolled down her cheek. She got up and left the table, walked into her room, shutting the door behind her.

'Ruheen, come on. Okay, I'll have one or two. Just because you made them—open the door. I'm eating one now, it's really nice.'

She opened the door to let him in. 'Don't say anything, I don't want to talk about it, I want to sleep,' she said with tears rolling down her cheek, while he looked at her dejectedly.

A sullen-faced Aditya changed quickly, and walked towards the sofa with his pillow, before plonking down and falling asleep.

PART II

Miles Apart
2007

'It's hard to tell the difference between sea and sky, between voyager and sea. Between reality and the workings of the heart.'
—HARUKI MURAKAMI

16

A few weeks later...
One morning, Aditya flew in from Delhi after a three-day business trip and drove straight to work from the airport. He got a call from Vidya just as he was getting into a meeting.

'Hi, can I call you back?' he asked, walking into the conference room for another classroom session on strategy by Shikha Agarwal.

'Adi, please come to the Emergency Ward at Bombay Hospital. It's Ruheen, I can't explain anything now,' she said in a tense voice.

'Vidya, tell me what happened!'

'Get to the hospital, Adi. Get here now,' she said, hanging up. Aditya had tried calling her on his way to the airport in Delhi and also on his way to work after arriving in Mumbai. She didn't pick up, and he presumed that she was asleep.

Aditya felt the ground beneath him shake. *What had happened to Ruheen?*

She had stayed at home all day for the past couple of months. She baked a few cakes, and had them delivered when she got orders. Sometimes she didn't take orders if she felt out of sorts and wasn't up to it. He got into his car, and navigated through traffic, to reach the hospital after an hour. He was told at the Emergency Ward that she had been shifted to a room in the General Ward. He ran across the corridor to room number 107 where he saw her covered in a white sheet, and sleeping like an angel. He sat down beside her, and ran his fingers over her cheek. Vidya walked in after a few minutes with a packet of medicines.

'Adi,' she said, 'I'm very sorry,' she wrapped her arms around him and rested her head on his shoulders.

'What happened, Vidya? Why is Ruheen here? Will someone tell me what is going on?' he said, sounding flustered.

'They couldn't save the baby, Adi. You have lost your first child,' she said, looking into his eyes with sadness.

'No, this isn't happening! How did this happen? How could we have lost our baby, Vidya?'

'There was a complication, Adi. I came with Ruheen to the doctor on her last check-up. She was asked to take extra precautions with her diet,' she said, shaking her head with regret.

'It was her smoking, wasn't it? She continued to smoke behind my back even after she knew she was expecting,' he said bitterly, watching her lie there like an innocent child.

'Adi, get a grip! She has just lost her baby; it wasn't just your baby! Also, it isn't my place to say anything, but it isn't just her fault, in the same way as it isn't just her responsibility.'

'Come on, Vidya, you know how things have been at work! These have been challenging times for me. What am I expected to do?'

'These have been challenging times for her too; you know how insecure she is, given the past, and what she's been through. You should have been there for her, Adi! This isn't something she was supposed to do alone, was it? You were supposed to take care of her, you promised her that,' she said firmly, as he averted his gaze.

He turned and stalked out of the room. When he came back an hour later when Ruheen was up. She was still sedated, and stared at the ceiling with a blank expression on her face. Aditya wanted to apologize to her, hold her in his arms and tell her that everything would be okay, but he held back. He was brooding and in his mind blamed her for what happened. A part of him began to believe that she had intentionally got rid of the baby, little realizing that it was stress she couldn't deal with.

'How did this happen, Ruheen? Why didn't you tell me that you have been having problems?' he said, trying not to be accusatory.

'Please Aditya, just leave me alone,' she said, turning on to the other side and closing her eyes. He leaned closer and stroked her hair, but she refused to acknowledge his presence in the room. The next day, she was discharged from the hospital and the two of them drove home in silence.

The next few days were extremely difficult. Ruheen spent most of her days in bed, crying about what had happened, and they spoke very little. Ruheen and he were advised to go for counselling, and discuss their problems. Both of them did go, but this didn't help them very much as neither of them was willing to get off their high horse and communicate.

There was a phase, two weeks after the miscarriage, when Aditya made a lot of effort, but she stayed away from him and shut him out, spending the entire day in the bedroom while he slept on the couch.

'Please leave me alone, Adi,' she pleaded. 'Don't you have a number of emails on your BlackBerry to answer?' She was spiteful and bitter, and in her mind the blame rested squarely with him.

Then there was a phase where Aditya did the same thing. She calmed down a bit after a few weeks, and would call him while he was at work, wanting to talk and spend time, but he encouraged her very little. Every time he saw a little baby in his business division's diaper advertisement campaign, he felt angry with her.

Ruheen found it extremely difficult to focus her energies on work. She enrolled into a fitness centre and also decided to take up yoga classes, but she found that she was not up to either. She spent most of her time watching television, reading a book or sipping tea and smoking a cigarette on her balcony.

She cut down her regular stream of supplies to Banyan Tree Café, citing health problems. She also began to refuse the occasional order that came her way.

One morning while she lay on the couch and read, her phone rang.

'Yes, this is Ruheen Oberoi,' she said.

'We need a 4-kg Dark Seductions cake for my sister's wedding at the Marriot. Could you please have it ready by this Sunday? We really like your selections,' the caller said.

'I'm sorry, I'm, unfortunately, going to be away this weekend,' she said with some hesitation.

'Are you sure? Do you think there might be some way?'

'I'm sorry, my best wishes to your sister and the family. Maybe some other time, thanks,' she said, hanging up.

A few minutes later, her phone rang again.

'Where are you going away this weekend? That was my colleague who called you, I spent ten minutes convincing him that your cakes are the best option,' said Vidya, sounding annoyed.

'I'm not up to it, Vidya. I don't feel like it! I don't feel like doing anything, I'm not sure about anything any more,' she said.

'Ruheen, calm down, please. You need to be strong and get back up on your feet. What are you doing next weekend?'

'Nothing, Adi is probably going to be in Kolkata for some shampoo launch.'

'Let's just get away for the weekend, just you and I. My boss has a place at Alibaug; I could get to use it for the weekend. How does that sound? *Chal*, you need a break, yeah?'

'Let me think about it,' she said, hanging up and going out to the balcony with her pack of cigarettes.

17

A month later...

Aditya was on a flight to Paris to discuss an important brand extension deal, along with the new marketing and communications manager of the company, Malika Kapoor, a young divorcee who had recently moved from Pune to join Aditya's team. Coincidentally, she was a year junior to him during his MBA, though they only knew each other vaguely back then. Now, they got on very well with each other and had grown to build a good working relationship. Aditya was fond of her, and she was one of the key people on his team who looked up to him. Aditya stayed absorbed in his copy of *The Economist,* while Malika, sitting opposite him, read a paperback.

'It was nice meeting your wife Ruheen at the office dinner,' Malika said.

'We aren't married, at least not yet. But yes, we had to head home early as she was a bit under the weather.'

'Yes, I heard so from Nikhat. It must be tough on her, losing her first child...'

'It is, but hopefully it'll be okay,' Aditya said looking tense. *If only she hadn't smoked so much during her pregnancy,* he thought.

She noticed that he seemed uneasy, and guessed the couple were going through a rough patch.

'I heard you and Ruheen were once together, you split up, and then with a twist of fate you bumped into her at Amsterdam,' Malika said emphatically, handing him her empty glass.

'Yes, it was strange and mystical. It seemed like it was destined to happen, I mean what were the odds...'

Good afternoon everyone, this is the Captain. We are flying at an altitude of 33,000 feet above sea level. We are flying over Munich in Germany and we are an hour and thirty minutes away from our destination. I hope you enjoyed your lunch and you are being well taken care of by Natalie and her crew. Sit back, relax and enjoy the flight. Thanks for choosing Air France and we hope you'll fly with us again very soon.

Time had flown by for Malika and Aditya very quickly. Malika listened intently to Aditya's story, about him meeting Ruheen back in college and again by chance in Amsterdam.

'All right, so you guys did hook up finally in Amsterdam?' she asked ecstatically while pulling out a blanket to cover herself.

'Yes we did,' Aditya said with a smile.

Malika and Aditya took a break for lunch, digging into the three-course meal being served by the flight crew.

After a short while Aditya asked, 'So what really happened between you and your ex-husband? What went wrong?'

'His bank called on the landline at home, checking if they should process a credit card transaction for a sizable bill at a club in Thailand. Unfortunately for him, they couldn't get through to his mobile number. He was supposed to be in Singapore for a banker's conference. These trips had been going on for two years of our married life, and possibly even before that. Of course, his mother blamed me for everything.'

'I'm sorry to hear that.'

'It's okay, the hard part started afterwards. I moved from Pune to Mumbai last year, and began my career from scratch at the PR agency. It was tough initially because I sat at home for two years after my marriage.'

'I can imagine; it must have been difficult,' he said with empathy.

'It is, given the magnitude of his deceit. I realize that on any given day he was shacking it up with other women, apart from having me around in his life. It makes me feel terrible to think that I'm not good enough despite putting in so much in the relationship.'

She noticed Aditya taking his gaze away from her and looking blankly at the screen before him, his mind far away, possibly reflecting on his own mistakes and missteps in life.

'Hey look here Adi, it really looks beautiful,' she said, looking outside the window. The aircraft was flying over a patch of greenery surrounded by hills. The landscape looked stunning and it made Malika envy the people who called such a beautiful land their home. *Parts of India are stunningly beautiful too*, she thought. Aditya drew closer towards her, leaning into her seat and looked over her head at the scenery below.

Please strap on your seat belts and put your seats in an upright position. We will be landing in Charles de Gaulle Airport in twenty minutes. The temperature in Paris is a pleasant 24 degrees and the time 4.45 p.m. Flight crew, back to your stations please, thank you.

'Adi, I want to know how things have been since Ruheen and you started living together.'

'We'll talk about it, but not discuss that now. Look at the view from here, it's breathtaking! You can see the Eiffel Tower in the far distance,' he said.

She followed where his finger was pointing and stared fascinated, wishing for a moment that she could go to the Eiffel Tower with him. A smile came to her face as his day-old stubble poked her bare shoulders.

18

The same day…

They reached the hotel in twenty minutes and it took an hour to sort out the confusion that they were not a couple and that they needed two single rooms.

'I'm sorry, sir, we've only got a suite available, which has been booked for you.'

'Can't you do something about it?'

'No, sir, I'm afraid we're fully booked.'

'Can we get a hotel somewhere nearby?' Aditya asked nervously. They had to be at an important meeting in two hours. Malika was meanwhile on the phone with the office in India, checking if something could be done, and another room arranged.

'It's the World Economic Congress in Paris tomorrow, sir. There are delegates from over 150 countries, media from all over the world and over 20,000 protesters in the city. Every good hotel in town is fully booked for the next three days.'

'Damn, what are we supposed to do?' Aditya said.

'We will let you have the Honeymoon Suite, sir,' said the slick front desk manager with his long gelled hair and toothy grin, almost giving Aditya a wink.

'We'll take it,' Malika said from behind, before Aditya could protest. 'It's all right, dude, I don't get to sleep in Honeymoon Suites every day, and I'm totally okay with it.'

'Why don't you go get ready first? I need to call Ruheen and check if she's okay. Damn, how could the office mess up our hotel reservations?'

'Chill, Adi, I need you to do me a favour.'

'What's that?'

'Come with me to the Eiffel Tower this evening...' she said looking at him with a gleam in her eyes.

'Let's see. Go get ready first,' he said, furiously punching away numbers on his BlackBerry.

Later, in the cab on their way to the meeting, Aditya turned to her as she gazed at the sights in Paris.

'Okay, yes we can go to the Eiffel Tower. I also know a nice French café very close to the Tower. We could go to the Moulin Rouge for dinner and some entertainment after that. Let me work on getting a table—Ruheen and I went there last year.'

'Aah...Ruheen is one lucky woman. Ten minutes don't pass without a mention of her,' she said, feigning jealousy. *Or was she actually jealous?*

'Yes, I realize that I keep bringing her up...' he said, knowing that it was almost impossible. *Ruheen is too much a part of me, it's like a part of her lives within me, he thought.*

'*Arrey,* it's okay, *baba!* I'm kidding; you can keep talking about her. It's very interesting,' she said pushing locks of hair behind her ears. To Aditya, for a moment there she seemed like Ruheen and not Malika, in the way she smiled at him.

'Hey, dude, why are you giving me that funny look?'

'Nothing, I just remembered something.'

'Or someone? Here we go again!' she said, slapping his arm affectionately.

■

Later that evening, they got ready one after the other and left for Eiffel Tower together. Malika looked fetching in a daring red dress that showed off her long legs. She had made an effort to dress up and the result was more than satisfactory.

'You look beautiful,' Aditya said, thinking, *you better keep yourself in check.*

'You don't look too bad in that sweater and your jeans, your stubble gives you a rugged look Mr I'm-so-lost-without-Ruheen,' she said with a flirtatious smile, while the concierge arranged for a taxi.

He got into the car wondering why fate was testing him like this. *What am I doing in Paris with this beautiful girl, while Ruheen is back home waiting for me?*

Aditya and Malika left in a rush, and urged the cab to get them to Eiffel Tower quickly. Malika couldn't believe that they were sharing the same suite, though it was her choice. To her, Aditya seemed too nice a guy to take advantage of the situation. She noticed that he looked dapper in a body-fit sweater and a pair of blue jeans which fit him perfectly.

'I really like your shoes,' she said, looking down at his feet.

'I picked them up in Amsterdam a couple of years ago—they're Ruheen's favourite,' he said with one of his half smiles.

'We're here,' he said cheering up a little, after a short drive from their hotel.

'It's beautiful,' she said gingerly, gaping at the Eiffel Tower with her head outside the window.

The two of them took the elevator up to the top and spent quiet moments staring out into the distance with a view of the beautiful city around them. Given that it was a weekday, there weren't many people up there. They noticed a few couples enjoying intimate moments, oblivious to the world around them. Some toddlers ran around with their parents behind them, making sure that they didn't fall. They stood silently, watching the sky grow from a light blue shade to shades of orange, red and then purple before it turned a shade of grey-black and the stars came out. Malika moved closer towards where Aditya stood, watching the nightlights in the city and reflected about her day so far till Adi interrupted her, 'Malika, do you want to leave? We have a reservation at the Moulin Rouge at 9 p.m. In traffic it will take at least thirty minutes to get there.'

'Yes, let's go, Adi,' she said, turning to see him smiling at her with confusion in his eyes. She had a sudden wish that he would take her in his arms and kiss her. She tried to get these thoughts out of her head, wondering if he could read her mind as his smile turned into one of his blank expressions.

They managed to put the awkwardness aside and had a nice evening at the Moulin Rouge. 'I love the colourful costumes and the dancing. It is a once-in-a-lifetime experience,' Malika said cheerfully. Aditya however, was lost in one of his deep, dark thought, back in his memories of a distant past. It didn't seem like he could let go, and he only managed to smile politely and kept up a brave face through the evening. He remembered his trip with Ruheen last year. He thought about the child they had lost; a loss that both of them were still dealing with, trying to repair their fractured relationship.

Once they got back, he changed into an old T-shirt and a pair of shorts quickly, and made his bed on the comfortable couch. 'We have to be at the airport by 7 a.m. I'll wake up at 5 a.m., get ready and then wake you up by 6. Let's target to leave by 6.30,' he said to her in a sleepy voice.

'Yes, boss,' she said, walking up to him. She put her arm around his neck and kissed him on his cheek, while he looked flustered.

'Thanks for being a sport, I had fun tonight. I would have been miserable alone,' she said, imagining how it would have been standing alone on top of the Eiffel Tower.

'I had a nice time, too,' he managed. 'You made my day a little less miserable than it could have been.'

'Adi, why do say that?' she asked, getting cross with him. 'I'm here all evening with you, and you can barely brace a smile. You are acting like someone has died ever since we got into Paris. Why were you so miserable all evening? What happened?'

'Nothing, get some sleep. We'll talk tomorrow morning. I'm glad you had a nice time; and sorry if I dampened your mood a bit. I didn't intend to,' he said with some regret. *Someone did die, it was my first child.* Ruheen and he hadn't spoken much for days.

'No, that's all right, you sleep well. You have four hours of sleep to catch up on, I'll see you in the morning,' she said, walking into the bedroom to change.

'Malika,' he called out.

'Yeah?'

'Hey, please go and change in the bathroom. You'll tempt me to come and watch, with you changing in the bedroom with the lights on,' he said with a laugh, while her ears went red with embarrassment as she unhooked her bra.

'Yeah, that's what I'm waiting for, you can help me if you like,' she said, knowing it was too much to ask from someone like him. She came to the conclusion that Aditya probably took Ruheen's permission before he kissed her. She half wanted to go in there in her sexy night dress and kiss him goodnight, but something inside her held back. She wanted him to make the first move.

'Ha ha, right. I'm really tired and sleepy, goodnight,' he said in friendly voice while she got into bed with a fashion magazine she had picked up at the concourse.

Aditya twisted and turned but sleep eluded him. Despite being up for over twenty-four hours, he was too disturbed and confused to fall asleep. He had been aloof and cordial with Malika all evening, at the risk of depressing her. He didn't like behaving as he did; putting on an icy demeanour and making little conversation at dinner, but certain things were hard not to remember and were difficult to move past.

He remembered that the evening with Malika in Paris was exactly the way Ruheen and he spent an evening in Paris, last year, on her twenty-fifth birthday.

Maybe I should have waited that night, he thought. *Life may have turned out differently then.*

19

A few weeks later…

Aditya got out of the shower and began to get dressed in a hurry. He had just flown in from Hyderabad, to attend his colleague and friend Nikhat's wedding. He noticed Ruheen, who was ready and waiting for him, sitting at the dressing table looking upset. She looked beautiful in a grey-blue sari. Tears were running down her cheek and she had smudged her mascara on her face.

'Ruheen, what happened? You're looking beautiful, love,' he said, walking up to her. 'We are running really late. The nikah is at 7 p.m. and it's already past 6…'

'I'm not up to it, Adi. I don't want to go.'

'Come on, you're looking great. Nikhat won't feel nice if you don't come. Besides, the change will do you good. Anuj's wife, Aparna, will also be there. You girls get along well; it will be a nice change for you.'

'I said I'm not up to it, I don't want to go,' she said, wiping the tears off her face. She began to remove her earrings and her necklace and put them back in the jewellery box, while Aditya stood there looking at her, helplessly.

'Not up to it? This doesn't work, Ruheen. This is the little time we get to spend together, and you're making a fuss. How can we get over what happened if we don't make an effort?'

'Yes, right. The little time we spend together is because of me, is it? I'm here day and night, in your house, within these four bloody walls, waiting for you. I'm always waiting,' she said, with tears rolling down her cheeks.

'I won't go either, I'll apologize saying that I missed my flight,' he said, walking up to her and putting his arms around her. 'Let's do whatever you want to do. You're gorgeous, my love, do you know that?'

'Yeah sure, just saying that doesn't matter. We need...I don't know.'

'I'm here now, like I said, let's do whatever you want to do.'

'Please go, Adi. I'm okay, I just need to be by myself,' she said, getting out of his embrace and picking out a matching tie for him.

'I'll leave soon after dinner, and I should be home by 10 p.m. Can I order something for you?' he asked.

'No thank you, have fun,' she said, walking into the bathroom and shutting the door behind her.

Aditya got into his car and dialled Malika's number. 'Have you left for the wedding already?' he asked.

'Hey, no, I'm just getting ready. What about you?'

'Good, can I pick you up then? Let's go together for the reception. Ruheen isn't coming so I could use the company.'

'Sure, I'll be ready waiting for you. Call me when you're downstairs.'

'Okay,' he said, driving out of his gate. He felt guilty about spending a lot of time with Malika, but she understood him and gave him a shoulder to lean on.

He got back early that night to see that Ruheen was already asleep. Instead of sleeping on the couch, he got into bed next to her, and went to sleep with his arm around her.

■

Their relationship continued to remain tense over the next couple of months. Ruheen felt bitter towards him, while he felt wronged and annoyed by the way she treated him. In the four and a half months since their return from Amsterdam, their relationship had steadily worsened. This is when Mohan and Vidya intervened. The four of them took a short holiday to Sri Lanka. It was out there that the frostiness between Ruheen and Aditya started to thaw; they both decided to put their egos aside and confront each other. They began to realize that they had problems and it was important that they talked things out, before things reached a point of no return.

'Do you think we can honestly make it last?' she asked. 'I'm very insecure, Adi, and I can't deal with this. I can't deal with you not being around for me. It kills me, it's like I'm not important!' she said, sitting at a little shack by a secluded beach.

'But you know it isn't like that! These few months weren't about you; it was about the stress with the changes at work. You know everything, Ruhi!'

'Exactly! What about me, Adi? These last few months should have been about me, but no! It was about you, your work, about the growth in your company. I'm so sick of hearing about it.'

'It's also about building a future. I put myself through a lot so that you and the baby could have a better future.'

'Yes, I don't deny how hard you work. But that shouldn't be at the cost of our today. Where are you when I need you?'

'I'm here, I don't know why you continue to feel this way. I know I should have been around more often…'

'Yes, you should have. I've had to bear the brunt of your work and your stress over hair oil and hair gel and diapers…'

'Yes, diapers too,' he said, looking into her eyes. Both of them looked at each other for a moment and smiled.

'I'll work on it, Ruhi. I want to work at it! Some of what happened was your fault, and much of it was mine. I'm just saying there is no reason for you to be insecure, there's nobody in my life as important as you. But we can move past this, I'm sorry,' he said, taking her hand in his. She looked at him with those intense and vulnerable eyes while they walked back to their cottage.

After they made love, Ruheen wrapped her arms around him and said, 'Do you know that it has been something like ten weeks since we made love?'

'We shouldn't wait so long, should we?' he asked, running his fingers through her hair playfully.

'No,' she nodded, with mischief and passion in her eyes, and held on to him tight before falling into a deep sleep.

20

After a month…

Aditya got home early on a Friday evening, and walked in to see Ruheen sitting on the couch, wrapped in a quilt, engrossed with an episode of *Lost* on television. Seeing him enter, she got up and walked up towards him with a glitter in her eyes. She wore an old sweatshirt of his and nothing else. Wrapping her arm around his neck and ruffling his hair she said, 'Why do you have a smirk on your face?'

'Aw, it's nothing, I'm just happy to see that look in your eyes. A few months ago it was a look of disdain and indifference,' he said quite foolishly.

'Shut up, Adi! Don't spoil it!' she cooed.

'I won't!' he said, picking her up in his arms with force and carrying her to the bedroom.

'Brute! Wait a minute, *na*, let me turn off the telly.'

'Nah, it's all right. We'll shut the bedroom door; there will be less noise filtering through.'

Thirty minutes later, while they lay with their arms around each other in bed, he gazed at her with an impish grin.

'There, it's that smirk again! What's up, Adi? You have to tell me,' she said, climbing on top of him.

'We need to shower, pack and head to the airport in an hour; we're flying out to the Maldives tonight. Tomorrow's my birthday, right? I thought we'll bring it in with the sound and smell of the ocean.'

'Oh Adi, I love you! That's a wonderful idea. Now let's hurry up! We have very little time.'

'Pack light, you don't have to carry all your lotions, perfumes and creams. It's just the weekend,' he said, rubbing her bare back.

A little while later, as they were rushing out of the apartment with their bags, her phone rang.

'Hi, yes, it is Ruheen. Yes, I remember you. Can I call you back? I'm on my way to the airport…what? Are you serious? Okay, I'm coming…I'll be there as soon as I can…' she quivered. Aditya watched her go pale as he walked towards her.

'Who was that, Ruhi?' She turned around and collapsed in his arms and started sobbing. Once she gained her composure, she said, 'Nana has had a stroke, he's pretty serious, Adi!'

'Okay, forget the Maldives, let's try and get a flight to Delhi or Chandigarh, and then a connecting one to Shimla. Don't worry, he'll be all right Ruhi.'

Ruheen packed some more clothes and they left for the airport in a sombre mood. He tried to reassure her as much as he could, but she struggled to maintain her composure. The flights to Chandigarh were fully booked and those for Delhi were full for the next couple of days. Aditya managed to put Ruheen on a business class seat on Air India. She was to take a flight to Shimla on a smaller regional airline.

'I will join you in the next few days, depending on his condition,' he said. They parted at the airport with a hug and a sloppy kiss.

'Thanks, Adi, I'm sorry I have to go away like this!' she sai,d feeling horrible about cancelling on the weekend he had planned.

'Sshh, don't say anything! It's the right thing to do. He's all the family you have…'

She kissed him again, and walked away swiftly into the departure terminal towards the check-in counter. Aditya took a cab back home and spent the next few hours sipping whisky and listening to U2 and Mark Knopfler.

■

He received a message from her when she landed in Delhi and another one the next morning when he woke up, 'In Shimla, at the hospital. He's stable now; the left side of his face and his left arm is paralysed. He is terribly weak, Adi!'

She called him a few minutes later, wishing him on his birthday, while he asked her to spend as much time as she could with Nana. 'He needs you by his side now, it might help him recover. I will get there as soon as I can take some time off from work,' he said.

Aditya soon realized that this was easier said than done. Days ran into weeks and weeks into months; three months to be exact. The Chairman supported by the Board of Directors, replaced Sakshi with him as the Head of the personal care products division. The last two quarters under her leadership were disastrous, and the business press was having a field day dissecting her quotes and pulling her apart on her missteps at managing the personal care products division. She was way too young and too inexperienced to be in the position she occupied.

For starters, Aditya took a decision to sell the Fresh brand to an MNC, who after the acquisition held a collective 30 per cent market share. With Bubble and now Fresh in their stable, Dentia Products took a strong third position in the market, leaving little room for anyone else to enter and start a price war like Indiana Products had two quarters ago.

This gave his division the ability to focus on their core, which was Engima and the range of hair care products. Aditya expanded the Enigma range, introducing a range of hair sprays, hair mousses and a range of premium shampoos sold in collaboration with a few leading salons nationwide. With the help of Enigma in Europe, they also began toying with the idea to introduce a range of aftershave gels, lotions and moisturizers that were doing very well in Europe.

Aditya began an 'Enigmatic Men' campaign with Rahul Kapoor and Rahil Khan, and began test-marketing the products in identified clusters. His product development team was working overtime to get this ready and out in a few months. This was a challenging task as his division was still infested with a number of people who were Sakshi acolytes, people with suspect capabilities and lacking the wherewithal to get things done. Aditya was forced to get rid of a number of people, motivate the capable naysayers and bring in a few whom he believed could do the job. These were remarkably stressful times, and many people among the competition, the media, and present and former employees of the company wanted to see him fail.

■

21

Ruheen walked into the ward where Nana had been admitted. She saw him sleeping with a number of tubes attached to his arm; he was being given a drip. She drew up a chair and sat beside him, putting her hand on his.

'They moved him to this ward last night, he's stable now,' a voice behind her said.

'Varun!' she said, turning around with surprise. She saw a tall, lanky guy with an athletic frame, standing in front of her.

'Ruheen Oberoi,' he said, with a faint smile. It appeared as if he hadn't slept all night.

'How bad is he? What are the doctors saying?' she looked at him with searching eyes, stressed out and upset.

'He's possibly lost the use of his left arm and the left side of his face. At his age, it could have been worse,' he said, trying to sound positive.

'Thanks for being here and taking care of him, Varun,' she said.

'No thanks needed, he's been my best buddy. We've been chilling together for a year now, since I moved back to Shimla.'

'I didn't know you were back! Gosh, it's been what, ten to eleven years since I last saw you. When did you get back?'

'Yes, something like that. I got back a year and half ago, a few months before my Nana passed away. I told him not to mention it, I've been keeping a low profile,' he said, sipping from the tiny cup of Nescafe he held.

'Oh okay, I'm sorry, I didn't know about your Nana,' she said. She got up and walked towards him.

'I'm sorry about your baby. The Major General took it quite

badly; he was very disturbed by the news, and very worried for you, of course.'

'You knew about it,' she said, lowering her voice and turning to gaze at her Nana.

'I did—he speaks about you all the time,' he said, 'when he's not talking about the war stories of course.'

'Yes, he does go on about that like a tape recorder, doesn't he?' she said, turning to look at her grandfather. She ran her hand stroking the scanty hair on his otherwise bald pate and kissed her Nana's forehead.

'Let me take you home, why don't you freshen up and settle in? You've travelled all night. We can come back to the hospital later in the afternoon; the doctor says he's likely to be up by then. He's sedated now.'

'Okay, let's go,' she said, picking up her bag and walking out of the private ward behind him.

'Ruheen, I'm sorry about eleven years ago,' he said, as they drove towards her Nana's estate, 300 metres above the hotel property his family had owned for generations.

'Oh okay, don't worry about it. It was so long back, we were kids, it seems like ages ago,' she said. Her thoughts were back home wondering what Aditya was doing. She also remembered her last trip to visit her Nana.

'What do you do these days? How come you're in Shimla? I thought you were managing the family business back in Bangalore,' she said with some curiosity.

'I'm running the family business here now, the hotel, I mean. Well, that's a long story, we can talk about that later,' he said.

■

Eleven years ago…in Dehradun
Varun pulled Ruheen along behind the stage, towards the dormitory behind the pine trees. They giggled as they disappeared from the crowd,

their voices muffled by the loud music from the rock concert a few metres away.

'I regret not being in the same school as you,' he said as he led her through the woods, holding her hand.

'Varun, I'm getting scared; what if there are snakes here, or some hungry leopard?'

'Chill, this isn't Nainital; there aren't any leopards in our school campus. What if we're spotted if we walk towards the boys' dormitory, especially with you in that school uniform of yours?'

'Yes, that's why I'm scared! Varun, if I get caught, I'm dead. I want to go back, yeah?' she said pleadingly.

'Come on, just for a little while.' He put his arms around her and kissed her on her lips. 'I really like you, Ruheen. You're hot! You're the most beautiful girl I've seen. I've liked you since the first day…'

'Dude, you used to call me motor mouth! You chased me away when I came to play with you,'

'You wore braces back then. You look great now, look at those legs,' he said, before he kissed her at the nape of her neck. They crept silently towards the back entrance of the dormitory.

'Shut up! You realize all this because you see me at your school's festival. What if I wasn't here? You would be saying the same shit to someone else.'

'Give me a break, there are so many other nice girls here, but I'm with you, na? I even broke up with both my girlfriends of three months for you. Because I couldn't take my eyes off you,' he said with a straight face as they hurried up the old staircase and rushed down the corridor towards his room.

'I broke up with my boyfriend too,' she said with a smile.

'He looked like a fool anyway. How did you end up with Mr Bones?'

'Shut up, you have a mean sense of humour. He plays the guitar,' she said, turning her nose up in the air.

'He didn't deserve a doll like you. A girl like you should be treated *like a lady. Besides you can listen to all the songs you want on my Walkman,' he said with a snicker. He turned on the lights of his room and shut the door behind her. He took out a box of chocolates from his cupboard and a card and gave it to her. 'I went to the Mall this morning, while you were busy in your painting competition.'*

'Oh, Varun,' she said, as they eased back on his bed and kissed each other. 'You're my first kiss,' she said, beaming. He ran his hand up her legs and kissed her on her neck. He fumbled with the hook of her bra, at which she laughed and helped him unhook it. They undressed and lay in his bed, kissing each other passionately, while Varun ran his hands all over her body, and gaped at the swell of her breasts with wonder.

There was a loud knock on the door. 'Ruheen Oberoi, open the door,' the voice said. There was more knocking and threatening till Ruheen and Varun got dressed hurriedly and opened the door to see her headmistress, the school captains and his warden standing before them, with looks that ranged from anger to disgust.

Ruheen was led away, and driven back to her school in Nainital the next morning. She was expelled from school the following week, which led to her Nana's second heart attack. Varun, on the other hand, after being pushed against the wall and slapped around by the warden, was let off with a final disciplinary warning, given that he had six months to go before his final exam.

■

Ruheen and Aditya spoke every day, if they could. Sometimes they spoke once in two or three days. A couple of times, he had tickets booked to fly into Delhi and onwards to Shimla but he couldn't make it and had to cancel. Nana's condition had improved considerably, and then got worse again after a few weeks.

Three months after Ruheen first left, she came back for a couple of days to pack more clothes and head back to Shimla. The doctors had said that her Nana had between a few weeks to three months to live. Ruheen and Aditya decided that it was important for her to be with him and to see him through to the end. Communication between them had begun to grow difficult, over the past three months, given the long distance. Though they got on and there were no open differences between them, there was tension beneath the surface. Aditya was more stressed out than ever, and was irritable given the situation at work with increased responsibility and his back against the wall. He had too much at stake. It was like being under a scanner and being asked to prove himself on a daily basis. In a way, he had asked for it. He didn't expect an easy ride when he replaced the daughter of the Chairman for the top job. Raman, his CEO, was waiting with bated breath to trip him up and replace him with one of his loyalists.

Meanwhile, Ruheen had a grouse against him, and rightly so, that he hadn't made a single trip in three months to see her Nana, and also that he went back to having very little time for her. Aditya did try, but it did seem impossible to make the time. He was traversing continents, trying work experiments out on the development front, for the products they were to launch. He spent more time in airports, on flights and in office till the wee hours of the morning than back home. He often went home to catch a few winks, shower and change. He walked in one day and was surprised to see her in the kitchen.

He walked up to her and put his arms around her waist, 'I've missed you so much, it's great that you're back. I'm not going anywhere for the next couple of days.'

'If you missed me so much, you should have come to Shimla, Adi! I don't understand, how, despite the fact that you're in a senior position, how difficult it is for you to take a couple of days off and come down,' she said, looking annoyed.

She turned around and looked at him with pain in her eyes. 'I'm confused, Adi! There are times when I need you by my side, and you're not around. You're too busy growing market share, and peddling hair gel for someone else,' she said chiding him.

'Ruheen baba, relax! I understand that you're upset, and rightfully so. It's just that this is a difficult and stressful time at work. I have everything to gain in the coming months and everything to lose.'

She fixed her gaze on him. 'Yes, you have everything to lose,' she muttered.

He kissed her on her cheek and whispered sweet nothings in her ear.

'You can't always say sorry and get away with it! Switch off both your phones, especially that BlackBerry and come to dinner.' She was still cross with him, and he ended up spending the rest of the weekend making it up to her. The fact that Nana was on his death bed didn't help matters.

22

The following month…

Aditya took a day off from work and flew with Ruheen to Chandigarh and drove down to Shimla. He managed to spend half a day with her Nana, reading to him by his bedside, which seemed to ease the tension between them.

'Ruheen, I'm putting the milk and eggs in the fridge. I did manage to pick up your Slim Milk too,' Varun said, walking into the kitchen. Ruheen and Aditya were sitting down and having a cup of coffee.

'Adi, this is Varun…' she said, as he turned around and looked at Varun with surprise.

'Shetty,' Aditya said, to which Varun turned around.

'Man, Aditya Sharma. I had no clue you were the Adi Ruheen spends hours talking about,' he said, turning his gaze on Ruheen. A familiarity now existed between them, and a growing bond of friendship as they nursed Nanaji and spent a lot of time together over the past few months.

'I didn't imagine you were the Varun she kept praising. The Varun Shetty I knew lived in a different world,' Aditya said, before embracing him.

'Well, my world has changed, I see yours has too,' he said, his gaze still on Ruheen.

'Yes, well, I can see we have a lot in common,' Aditya said.

'I think we do. Let's sit outside,' he said.

'You guys sit and talk, I need to serve Nana his soup, I'll be with you in a few minutes, with a cup of coffee for both of you,' Ruheen said.

Aditya and Varun sat outside in the balcony attached to the living room, which had spectacular views of the valley below. They watched the sun go down behind the mountains as the fog cleared for a few minutes, while they spoke about how Aditya and Ruheen met, and his stint at SK Products.

'I don't understand, how did you end up in Shimla? I know you have roots here, but why did you give up your interests in the distribution set up?' Aditya asked.

'You didn't hear the story?' Varun asked.

'No, nothing other than you sold out and left Bangalore.'

■

Varun's Story
'This incident took place almost a couple of years ago. It was a friend's birthday, and Mickey asked me to pick up his friend, Sakina from her place in Koramangala. We were to drive out to a private party at a farmhouse near Whitefield. I picked up this girl from her place; it was weird as she got into my car wearing a Muslim abaya. I wondered what Mickey was trying to pull off, but once we got onto Airport Road, she took it off, revealing a skimpy black number and a tattoo on her upper back. She quickly lit up a cigarette while I looked at her with confusion.

"What? My lunatic brother will kill me if he catches me wearing this! He can do what he likes, while I get treated like a prisoner."

I realized her brother was Sahil, notorious for his temper among the people I hung out with. Their family had varied business interests, from furniture stores to schools and hospitals. In any case, I was drawn towards her, she seemed interesting having returned from the US much like I did. She spoke about her interests in music, and how she was a part of a jazz trio, which her family was against.

A few hours later, while we were jiving on the dance floor, I felt someone nudging me from behind. It was Mickey. "Tell Sakina that her brother is here. I saw him at the bar while I was picking up drinks," he said in a hushed voice. I did tell her, which made her very worried.

We both slipped out through the main entrance and walked towards the car park which was some distance away from the farmhouse. We heard agitated voices behind us, asking us to stop, hearing which we began to run.

"Give me your car keys, let me drive," she said, taking them away from me.

"I got in next to her and we pulled out of the car park and rushed towards the main street. Both she and I were very drunk. Though I abstained, she had smoked a few joints earlier that night. She drove rashly towards the city as we were being pursued by her brother and his friends.

"Why can't you stop?" I said. "He knows you were at the party anyway."

"Dealing with this at home is easier than dealing with it on the streets," she said. She sped on, keeping her gaze on the rearview mirror, noticing them catching up with us. The rest of it is a blur— she seemed scared to death, and sped on like a woman possessed. At the junction near the flyover to Koramangala, she lost control and braked suddenly, skidding into a divider.

I woke up in the hospital the next morning. I was told that she had been killed on the spot; her family had met with mine and reached a settlement with the cops. The story spun to the media was that she was tipsy that night and had borrowed a friend's car to get home after a party. Neither her brother nor I were involved in statements made by the police. I was asked to stay quiet and keep out of the way while the "businessmen" managed the press, police and eye-witnesses. Weeks after her death, my half-brother made an offer to buy out my share in the family business. He believed that it was being affected by my reputation and rash ways, particularly when eye-witnesses revealed to the media in the following weeks that I was also involved in the crash, and that I was driven to the hospital by a private cab driver.

■

'As you know, I didn't have much of an interest in the business, especially so since my dad passed away a year before this accident. I was shaken by the whole incident—I felt responsible for letting her drive, especially given the inebriated state she was in. I decided to come here and spend some time with my ailing grandfather and evaluate what my life was about and how I wanted to live. He didn't last more than six months, but I'm glad I spent those six months with him. Since then, I've been refurbishing his heritage hotel and spending time with Ruheen's Nanaji. Our families go way back. Her grandfather and mine went to school together, and so did her mum and mine. They were together at Welham, and were the best of friends.

"She and I go way back, too, we had this childhood crush on each other, which unfortunately didn't work out. But you're a lucky guy, Ruheen's a sweetheart. Hang on to her…"

"She sure is, dude. Though I didn't know the two of you were connected," Aditya said in a contemplative voice.

"Yeah, well…it was a childhood crush, man. It wasn't a big deal."

"What are you guys talking about? Don't tell me Adi is telling you how to sell hair oil and such," Ruheen said, walking up to them with a tray that had three mugs of coffee and a plate of cookies.

"Yes, something like that," Varun laughed. "How is he?"

"He's fallen asleep," Ruheen said, moving close to Aditya and putting her arm around him.

"Okay, good. I'm going to finish this and call it a night, you guys must have a lot of catching up to do," Varun said.

"Stay, you can have dinner with us," Ruheen said.

"No, it's good, I'll see you tomorrow," he said, finishing his cup of coffee. "Let me know if you need a drop to the airport. It was good seeing you, *dost*," he said, shaking Aditya's hand.

"Thanks, likewise," Aditya said.

"Goodnight," Ruheen said to him, walking with him to the porch.

■

Ruheen and Aditya made love after over three months in her bedroom that night. Both of them stayed up pretty much all night talking about her childhood, her life in boarding school in Nainital and the holidays she spent in Shimla with her Nana.

'So you see, Varun was the reason why I got thrown out of school and went back to Shimla. That's also the reason why I chose to go to college in Mumbai and not Delhi. I knew from Nana that he went to college there. I didn't want to be anywhere close to him, I was so mad at him,' she said, sitting up and tying her hair in a bun, while Aditya gazed at her with affection.

'This Varun, are you sure he's okay?' Aditya asked, while rubbing her back.

'He now is. He's more at peace with himself,' she said, while thinking about the compassion he had shown her Nana since he got back. He would sit and play chess with him every evening and listen to the same war stories and days of the partition, over and over again.

'He was quite a wild child, back when I knew him. He was nice to me, but he had a reputation for being a junkie and womaniser.'

'I was once a wild child, too,' she said defensively. 'I don't blame him, given what he's been through. His mother was his dad's mistress. They were in love and couldn't marry, as he had already taken a wife. Over time she got depressed, and one day, left Varun outside his office, and eloped with some other guy. She married this other guy and left for Australia. Imagine Varun's life, being brought up by his dad who already had a family. He was always in boarding school or in college away from home. His older step-brother did everything possible to push him out of favour with the father. His Nana was the only one who gave him the love and attention he deserved,' she said.

'Hmmm, that's sad. Okay let's sleep. I have to wake up and leave at 7 a.m.,' Aditya said.

'No way!'

'Yes, I have an early flight out to Mumbai.'

'No Adi, you're staying for breakfast, period. Actually, it's more likely to be brunch. I don't think you'll get fired if you take a day off. You don't have an option,' she said, sounding like a spoilt child.

'Okay, I'll stay if it makes you happy.'

'It sure does,' she said, 'when are you going to be back?'

'I should be able to make it back for your birthday. In fact, I will be back,' he said.

She fell asleep with her arms wrapped around him tightly, like she was sure if she let him go, he wouldn't come back. Aditya took a cab to Chandigarh the next afternoon after bidding her a reluctant goodbye, promising to be back in time for her birthday in a month.

23

Two weeks later...

'Hey, he seems to be asleep,' Varun said, walking into the veranda, where Ruheen was sitting down with her feet up and reading an old classic.

'Yes, he is. The poor dear has been sleeping a lot lately. He barely eats, anyway.'

'So, how're things? What are you up to?'

'Nothing much, reading *A Tale of Two Cities*, not much to do. The servants take care of everything. How's it going for you?'

'Great, it's been busy. It's the first season since we renovated, business has started to pick up. We are near full occupancy.'

'That's wonderful,' she said, closing her book and sitting up. 'I've started putting on weight, sitting around here all day and doing nothing.'

'Come for a jog with me, the weather is good. I can wake you up at 7 a.m., every day. It's a nice run, with pleasant views.'

'Not a bad idea, wake me up tomorrow.'

'Ruhi, I hope you don't mind me calling you that, but do you feel like heading out? We could catch a film at the Mall and eat out, maybe.'

'I don't mind, it sounds better than being called motor mouth,' she said with grin. 'Yes, I'm bored to death, let's go. Give me ten minutes to change, maybe twenty.'

'Sure,' he said. It took his breath away when she came out fifteen minutes later, wearing a peach-coloured skirt and high heels.

'That's quite a transformation, you look stunning,' he said. 'Let's just go for a long drive and then head up to Wildflower

Hall for dinner. I don't want to cause a riot by taking you to the Mall, with you dressed like that. You'll end up becoming Shimla's latest tourist attraction.'

'Shut up! You still have your whacky sense of humour, some things never change,' she said, going red in the face.

'Yes, they don't, much in the same way as you still are drop dead gorgeous and, you still have a great pair of legs,' he said with a smirk.

'Stop Varun, you're making me feel self conscious! Let's go,' she said, as they walked together towards his black Octavia. He was taken in by her charm and the intoxicating fragrance she wore. He had to hold himself back, telling himself that she was in a committed relationship.

They sat at the terrace outside the café, with a view of the valley and neighbouring peaks, and with the sound of the chirping birds, interspersed with music, instrumental versions of 'Careless Whisper' followed by 'Unchained Melody' by Richard Clayderman filtering outside.

While at dinner, he looked at her with intense eyes, wondering what to say to her. He feared that she could sense that he was drawn to her, which could complicate their relationship.

'Thanks for pulling me out. I can't believe I'm sitting here with Varun Shetty, the boy who made me cry so much,' she said, smiling at him warmly.

'I'm sorry; it was insensitive to call you motor mouth.'

'Not that, stupid! I had this massive crush on you, and you ignored me. I used to do these caricatures of you and draw hearts all over and slip it under your door, but you never acknowledged it.'

'First, I didn't know you had a crush—this is interesting, let's come back to this one. Second, that was you? I thought it was that creepy guy who worked at the reception for my Nana. I got scared each time I saw the drawings, and think about how weirdly he would say "Hello, mere Varun Baba".'

'Ha ha, that's hilarious. I was surprised when you hit on me at that ill-fated school festival. I mean here was a guy who ignored my presence every summer…'

'For the record, sorry about everything, Ruhi,' he said earnestly.

'It's okay! Did you actually like me, or were you just fooling around? Tell me honestly,' she said, as they began to eat. 'You chased away a nice boy who serenaded me with the guitar, back then,' she said, pushing her hair behind her ear and digging into her pasta.

'I did really like you, I felt horrible about the whole thing. I wanted to meet you over summer and talk things out, but my dad didn't send me to Shimla, knowing that you would be there. He was mad at me, and sent me to do a part-time job at a local newspaper. I didn't date for the rest of the school year.'

'Wow, I kind of hated you for a while after that. It mainly had to do with what happened to Nana, but it's okay, it was silly what happened. I hated that school anyway, in hindsight it was good to come back and spend two years of school with Nana.'

'I was a bit down when I heard that you got married to some Rohan from London and left the country. Our grandfathers were doing all they could to set us up together,' he said.

'Yes, I know, wasn't that strange? It was like—hey, you played with that guy and you ended up kissing him back in high school, now go and marry him. Though, if I hadn't met Rohan, it would have happened. I had kind of accepted it, but you know life is unpredictable.'

'It is. You were with Aditya before that, weren't you?'

'Yes, that was another crazy phase, with that obsessive Vishal hounding us and threatening to hurt Aditya.'

'For some reason knowing both of you back then, I don't know what kind of a match you guys would have made. I mean, then, he was quite meek and kept to himself.'

'Yeah, it took two years for him to walk up and ask me out.'

'Not bad, it has taken me like eleven years, if we forget to count my rather inappropriate proposition of taking you to my dorm,' he said with a cackle.

'Ha ha, yes, you're funny. It has taken you eleven years to ask me out properly. Aditya was funny back then. In college, he would sit at the café, pounding away on his laptop with a frown on his face. Though every time I looked across the café, I caught his gaze and he was looking right back at me.'

'Yes, I guess he was shy or something. Did I tell you about the time I took him from one end of Bangalore to another to pick up weed from this seedy neighbourhood? He was mortified—you should have seen his face,' Varun said, sitting back and sipping on his iced tea.

'What are you saying ?' She looked at her phone screen, to respond to a text message from Aditya.

'Yes, he was quite uptight back then. He taught my receptionist the right telephone etiquette, he would complain about salesmen playing truant and going off for movies on a Friday. He was a real spreadsheet guy. I think he googled everything, I don't think he reads a book or watches a film before reading five reviews,' Varun said with a laugh.

'Yes, it's quite funny; he does it with restaurants as well. He says, "Let's not go here, *Timeout* gave it a two-star rating'. He even writes some reviews here and there. The other day he showed me some review he had written for a business hotel in London which got published in some magazine.'

'Wow, a man with an informed opinion, isn't he? Well, he lives in with you, which makes him a pretty cool guy,' Varun said with a friendly smile.

'Yes, I'm the difficult one now, telling him to hang his towel out to dry or nagging him to make the bed,' she said with half her attention on her phone.

'A movie doesn't sound like a bad idea, I'm sure they have a night show, do you want to go? There is the new Pixar animated flick called *Up*. We can buy you a lot of caramel popcorn too.'

'Oh, you remember that! I used to be nuts about caramel popcorn. Let me just call and check if Nana is okay and if he has eaten. It doesn't sound like a bad idea. What's it about?'

'It's about some old man, a chubby kid and a lot of balloons,' he said with a look of disbelief.

'Ha ha sounds perfect, you were quite the chubby one as a kid,' she said while calling her Nana's caregiver on his mobile phone.

'I was, actually I lost a lot of weight by the time we first hooked up, I was podgy till not long ago. But I'm all fit now,' he said with a wink.

'Okay, thanks for letting me know,' she said with a sheepish smile.

A few hours later, he dropped her back home and walked her up to the door.

'Thanks, Varun, I don't believe I've laughed so much in a long time,' she said before giving him a peck on his cheek and ruffling his spiky closely cropped hair.

'I'm glad you had a nice time. Sleep well and see you tomorrow,' he said. He watched her open the door and get out of the car.

'Ruheen, please try and smile more often. It looks great when you do. When does Aditya come back to the mountains?'

She looked at him with an impish grin and then turned her attention to her handset. 'Shit, I've had three missed calls from him. He should be back in a couple of weeks for my birthday, I guess. I'm going to go in, I'm feeling really cold,' she said, hugging herself.

'Sure, goodnight.'

She walked in and went up to her room with a smile on her face. Varun was sensitive and funny, he made her feel good about herself. He made her feel special; it was something she hadn't felt in a long time. She got into bed and dialled Aditya's number.

∎

After two weeks...
Ruheen came out into her balcony and sat by the sill, staring into the far distance, looking at the apple trees in the grove below and thinking about Aditya and life back in Mumbai. The gift she received from him by courier was lying unopened on the table next to her bed. She set her gaze on a bunch of rogue monkeys who jumped from tree to tree, who scared the birds out of the branches where they were perched. It was a clear blue sky, despite the nip in the air, and she enjoyed the view of the snow-clad peaks. She jogged her memory back to her childhood, when her Nana built her a huge snowman for her birthday. She had spent pretty much all day in bed. It was her birthday and she was in low spirits, as Aditya had to cancel his trip to Shimla at the last minute.

A week ago...
'Hi. Look, I've got to take a rain check on my trip to Shimla. This important meeting with the distributors has come up; I need to sort some things out. I'm sorry, I'm afraid it's unavoidable. I've got a series of back-to-back trips, with the launch coming up,' he said with a hint of worry in his voice.

'Hmmm...okay! Well, what can I say? It's not something I'm thrilled about,' she said, rage building up inside her.

'I'm sorry, all right? I'll make this up to you, I promise. Say hi to Nana from me, I'll talk to you soon.'

'Hmm...I hate you for doing this.'

'I hate myself too. But I love you.'

'Bye,' she said.

She realized that they had spent both his and her birthday apart. She tried to put it out of her mind, and began to think about her Nana who was getting weaker by the day. She heard him calling out to her.

'I'm coming, Nana,' she said, walking towards his room swiftly.

Neither her Nana nor Varun had remembered that it was her birthday, which put her off even more. Her Nana was among the first to wish her every year, whether she was in London, Mumbai or Amsterdam.

'Take me into the balcony. Not yours, the one in my living room,' he said gruffly, as she wheeled him out of his room.

She opened the door and stepped out pushing his wheelchair, to see the surprise of her life. She saw the balcony lit up, it was decorated with balloons and flowers. She saw Varun stand there in a casual blazer and pair of jeans grinning at her. 'Happy birthday, Ruhi!' Varun and Nana said at the same time. She bent down to kiss her Nana on his cheek, while he blessed her.

'The surprise isn't over,' Varun said, 'Girls, you can come in now.' Ruheen stared at him with curiosity and with a big smile on her face.

'Oh my God!' she said, seeing her closest friends from school, Priya and Samantha walk in. She hadn't seen them in over ten years. She ran across to hug them as they greeted her. She finally walked up to Varun and said, 'How did you manage this?'

'Not too difficult, everyone is on Facebook these days. The girls thought it would be a good idea. Both of them live in Delhi anyway so it wasn't too much of a journey for them,' he said.

'Thanks, Varun,' she said with a sparkle in her eyes.

'The surprise isn't over,' he said. He went over to the living room and came back with a guitar. 'Before the birthday girl cuts her cake, I'd like to play her a song or two. I'm glad that for the past year I've done one useful thing in my life—I've learned to play the guitar. I once deprived Ruhi of the company of this guy who serenaded her with the guitar. I guess today I get to make up for it,' he said with confidence as the girls cheered him on.

A while later, after helping her Nana into bed, and after dropping the girls back to their rooms at Varun's hotel nearby, Varun dropped Ruheen back to her place.

'Come up for a coffee on my balcony,' she said, 'It's still my birthday, two hours to go till midnight. I'd much rather stay awake through the rest of it.'

'Sure,' he said, before getting out of his car and following her in. They chatted over cups of coffee on her balcony and enjoyed the music that played on the speakers in her room, and spoke excitedly about the fun evening.

'It was fun to see your Nana cutting the cake along with you. It makes for a great picture,' he said, showing her the image on his digital camera.

'It's wonderful, I'll always remember it,' she said with tears in her eyes. 'How did you come up with all this? Why?'

'Because...I thought Aditya isn't coming, you're going to just sulk around and be unhappy.'

'But then it's his business to keep me happy. Why did you go out of the way? It's something I would expect him to do, not you,' she said teasingly.

'But I did it okay, Ruheen? I can't just stand there and see you being down in the dumps. I mean it's probably your last birthday with your Nana. You might as well look back at it and remember it as being a memorable birthday.'

'You're sweet, Varun, thanks,' she said with intensity in her voice, 'you do strum the guitar pretty well.'

'I dance pretty well too,' he said. 'Come waltz with me,' he said, before holding her by her hips and leading her into dance. They danced for a while as they drew closer together. Soft jazz by Miles Davis set the perfect mood for a slow waltz; he felt her breath on his cheek.

'I like this music,' she said softly, as she felt his fingers on the small of her back.

'Thought you were more into Nirvana and Def Leppard,' he said, as she moved her arms and placed them around his neck.

'That was eleven years ago, I'm a woman now, don't you realize?' she said dreamily.

'It is a long time, but a lot of things about you are the same,' he said.

His face turned towards her and looking deep in her eyes, he leaned in and kissed her on her lips, while she closed her eyes and kissed him back.

'I didn't mean to, I shouldn't have, I'm sorry!' he said, before tearing away from her embrace.

'I need to get some air,' she said and walked out of the room. She went outside into her little terrace.

He stood there thinking, *man I love her so much! What am I supposed to do now?*

Ruheen stood there, for a moment, trying to comprehend what just happened. She put her hand on her head and sat down on the swing with a look of confusion in her eyes.

24

After a week...

Ruheen walked into the Pleasant Villa Resorts property and asked for Varun at the reception. She was sent up to the suite he kept on the top floor.

'Is this where you live?' she asked, walking in. She was wearing a pair of old jeans and a kurta.

'Yes, I didn't need all the space we had; I converted that into a family suite, and took one of the smaller ones. It's a nice view from here,' he said, not looking at her.

'It sure is, err...I came to talk to you. What happened that night...'

'Look, I'm sorry, I shouldn't have. I made a mistake, it's just that we have this great chemistry and...anyway, it's wrong. You're with Aditya and I respect that,' he said with conviction.

'See, I don't want what happened between us to affect Nana. You've been spending an hour with him before I wake up and you leave. He spends the rest of the day asking for you. It doesn't mean you don't visit him or spend time with him.'

'Okay, look, don't worry, I'll be there. I just felt it awkward to be around you, but you're right, it shouldn't affect him. I'll see you tonight,' he said, before turning away from her.

'Varun, look, at me,' Ruheen said emphatically, 'It's okay. You're staying for dinner.'

'You're going to punish me with your cooking?'

'Yes, pretty much. That way you'll think twice before you kiss me next time,' she said in a familiar voice.

'Did you tell Aditya what happened? He's a good guy,' Varun

said with concern.

'He doesn't have to know. We have enough trouble already; we don't know where we're headed. He's too busy and I'm a little ticked off with his no show last week.'

'Take it easy, it's the long distance that's talking,' he said.

'Sometimes even in Mumbai, it feels like a long distance relationship,' she said with a look of dismay, before walking out.

■

Meanwhile
Malika kept to herself, and was unusually quiet during the flight to Amsterdam. She was put off by Aditya's aloofness over the past two weeks; she was also very tired, as she had slept very little. She looked pristine in a black V-neck top and a pair of faded Levi's jeans.

'What are your plans in Amsterdam after we finish our planned meetings?' Aditya asked. He realized that he had been tough on her, what with his mood being in the dumps because of his trouble with Ruheen. She turned her gaze towards him and looked at him intently.

'I have another meeting at 11.30 a.m. in Hilversum, one with the advertising agency. It's apparently twenty minutes away by train. Post lunch, I should be back. I aim to see a bit of Amsterdam before we leave in a couple of days,' she said, showing little emotion.

'Well, I could help with that. I've got nothing much to do after the conference that finishes at 6 p.m. tomorrow. What time do you fly out? I'm going to Munich after Amsterdam.'

'My flight is at 5.30, though I wish I could have stayed a bit longer. I have to get back and work on scheduling the events for the launch of Enigma in the Middle East.'

'That gives us enough time to see a few places. What do you feel like doing ? There are different things you could get up to in Amsterdam, you know…'

'Ugh, stop being gross! What do you imagine I would get up

to?' she said blushing, and smiling a little. She appeared to be in a pensive mood.

'I'm just joking, there are different things we could do. We could take a boat ride or visit a few museums and galleries or go shopping or just eat, drink and party.'

'Sounds interesting, we could mix it up. You make the itinerary; after all, you know the place much better than I do. But let's decide on this once I get back from my meeting.'

'Sure, let's do that. I've got the office to put me up at Rho Amsterdam, the same one I spoke to you about. It's close to Dam Square, and would make it easier. What about you?'

Her reservations were made a few days after his.

'I found a good hotel online, and got the office to make a booking. From the pictures it looks pretty interesting. It's a canalside hotel,' she said taking out her booking confirmation and showing him the address.

'That's great; this is ten minutes away from where I'm going to be. I've seen this place, Ruhi and I went down to a café opposite this hotel on my second trip to Amsterdam,' he said while getting out of the aerobridge and following her into the Arrival Terminal.

'How are things with Ruheen now?'

'Well, up and down. We haven't spent much time together of late. I've asked her to book her tickets and come to Mumbai next weekend. But it isn't looking very promising from what I can see.'

'I hope she does come, Adi,' Malika said less reassuringly.

In a short while, they walked out of the airport together. They took a taxi together and Aditya dropped her off at her hotel, promising to meet her there at 2 p.m. as they had planned to go for lunch.

25

Two weeks later...

Ruheen picked up her phone after the third ring; it was Aditya at the other end. She was sitting at the table and playing a game of chess with Varun, after Nana had been tucked in.

'Hi, yes I'm doing all right. What about you?' she asked.

'I'm okay, I leave for Amsterdam next week on an important trip, to get a deal finalized. I'm going to try coming up there, but I can't promise. Do you think you can make a trip down here for a couple of days?'

'Hmmm, no, I can't just leave Nana and come, not at this stage. He's really frail now; he just sits out on his wheelchair for a couple of hours. The rest of the time he's in bed, he's talking a lot less.'

'That's a pity, what is his doctor saying ?'

'Four weeks or less they say. Anyway, look I'm sitting here with Varun, I'll call you back,' she said, before hanging up and getting back to her game. Varun and she maintained a distance from each other, and spent a lot less time together than was the case in the past, given how he felt about her.

'I'm thinking about leaving Aditya,' she said carefully, as he looked up with surprise.

'He's a nice chap, work things out...' he said encouragingly.

'It's what you say all the time, Varun! I feel miserable in this relationship; I've been left alone every time I've needed him. When I lost my baby, when my business fell apart, now with Nana unwell...I've not had the kind of support that I need. His priorities are more about growing in his company, his career, the money he makes.'

'He must be feeling the pressure too. Look, I can imagine there are many people like him and you, going through the same problems.'

'But I don't get it, Varun, despite having everything, Aditya still clings on to things he doesn't believe in and a job he hates. In the bargain, I suffer, our relationship suffers.'

'It isn't easy to give it all up,' he said. 'Besides, I'm sure he has a good reason for what he does.'

'You have given it up, you're at least trying to live a life you believe in and has meaning beyond the mundane. You've stopped drinking and smoking, you've changed your lifestyle. You took the option of getting out and not being a part of the rat race. He isn't, he doesn't want to, despite us being together,' she said, sounding upset, walking across the room. 'It's like I'm not good enough, sometimes. I've been through a lot you know. He doesn't get it or he thinks it's easy to deal with coming out of an abusive relationship or losing my child. Do you know how stressed out I was before I lost my baby? I was supplying a cake for a wedding, when I spotted Vishal, coming out of the hotel. I dropped the cake and ran from the venue. I stayed at home for a week, fretting for my life…while Aditya was busy in Frankfurt on work.'

Varun sat there dumbfounded, listening to her unburden the problems she had been having. So far, she had bottled her feelings up and put on a brave countenance. It seemed to him that her relationship with Aditya was crumbling. He walked out a short while later in a sombre mood, worried about her, given the failed marriage and the miscarriage she had been through. Some *people face more than their share of problems,* he thought.

The next morning, he pulled her out and took her for a run with him. He felt that by keeping her occupied, instead of her sitting at home, he could make her feel better.

'You're right, this does feel good,' she said, walking up to the car behind him.

'Breakfast?' he asked.

'Okay,' she said, wiping her brow with a towel taken from the boot.

'India Coffee House?' he asked.

'Nice idea,' she said, getting into his car. He noticed that she was in better spirits; getting things off her chest seemed to have helped.

26

10 days back...

Malika managed to conclude her meeting by 1 p.m., and took the train back to Amsterdam from Hilversum. She sat back and enjoyed the short journey which offered a glimpse of a beautiful countryside that included old windmills out of a fairytale, pretty wooden cottages and colourful graffiti plastered on the walls near the station. Wearing a cheerful smile on her face, she walked into the hotel a few minutes past 2 p.m., to see Aditya sitting at the coffee shop in the lobby area patiently reading a book.

'Hey, did you miss me?' she asked saucily to which he looked up with a smile.

'Thanks for disturbing, I'm halfway through already,' he said. He was reading a book called *Netherland*. 'It's actually a story set in New York; it's a tale of friendship between an American of Dutch origin and a shady Trinidadian entrepreneur who bond over cricket. One of those post 9/11 books about life in the Big Apple.'

'You seem like you're enjoying it,' she said sitting down next to him.

'So what do you want to eat? What do you want to do this evening?' he asked sportingly. She looked at him appreciatively. He had made an effort to dress up, he looked smart in a polo T-shirt and pair of blue jeans. He had shaved after days and she was quite drawn by the fragrance of his aftershave.

'Well, I don't know. We had a late breakfast, besides I'm not really the type who would enjoy going to a museum to admire art and artefacts. Unlike you, I'm not a big fan of the Renaissance period. I think a boat ride sounds okay, but we could do that tomorrow morning. While we have some energy I would much rather go to the beach you spoke about.'

'You mean Zandvoort, near Haarlem? We'll have to take a train down there. Let's leave—we could grab a bite on the way to the station. I might need to pick up a pair of beach shorts too. I didn't bring any, didn't plan on visiting the beach.'

'Hang on, come up for a bit. Let me change, *baba*! I'm not coming to the beach wearing this skirt and a pair of stockings.' He followed her upstairs; he stood gazing at canal and the view of the church 500 metres away, while she changed into a swimsuit and wore on an old T-shirt and a pair of shorts.

'Nice tan,' he said looking at her legs, while walking out of the room. He was in much better spirits than when they had boarded the flight to Amsterdam.

'There's something about this place that lifts my spirits,' he said cheerfully.

'I'm sure…maybe it's the smell of weed,' she grinned.

'Yeah, you bet! Maybe that's what it is. Hang on, do want to eat hummus and pita bread, because the guy across the street serves it up nicely. It's also cheap and easy on the tummy.'

'Yep, I don't mind,' she shrugged as they walked across the street towards the eatery. A short while later, with their stomachs full, and after quickly picking up a funny green and orange pair of swimming trunks, they got onto a tram that took them to the station. The colour was back in Aditya's face and he no longer looked like a lost soul.

'I brought a book for you to read if you would like, *Of Mice and Men*—it's a classic.'

'I'm not much of a reader, but thanks. I'll give it a try if we run out of things to talk or do on the beach,' she said suggestively. For a moment he looked strange and aloof, but quickly recovered.

'We should have picked up a Frisbee too,' he said with a little laugh and added, 'It would be fun to see you trying to catch one.'

'I don't think that's such a good idea. Not after eating so much of hummus and pita bread, which was delicious by the way.'

'How did your meeting go? I forgot to ask,' he said as the train crawled into Haarlem, and both stood up to get off.

'Oh yes, it was good! We're sorted. We'll be doing two events here next month, one in Belgium and one in Paris. It was a breeze dealing with this event company. They are very professional and experienced. I'm quite optimistic about our success.'

'That's good then. I just met an old acquaintance from Enigma. Someone I knew when we first came here to strike a deal. We spent some time over coffee this morning. There's a positive buzz about the work we're doing, and about the variants we're launching in international markets. Anyway, I then went by to the bookstore and spent some time there,' he said as they walked to the town centre to rent bicycles.

'Do we have to rent bicycles?' she asked. 'Maybe we can take a cab or something. I mean it's past 4 p.m.'

'Don't worry, sunset at this time of the year isn't till after eight. Riding out there is half the fun. You'll enjoy the ride. It's only twenty minutes away, R...' He almost said her name and stopped himself. He wondered what she was doing right now. *She must have her head buried in a book or maybe she's playing a game of scrabble like every day.*

'Okay, yes, chief. As you wish. But if I fall you're to blame. I haven't ridden a bicycle in over ten years.'

'It's like swimming, one doesn't forget. Now pedal on, I'm behind you. I suggest you tie your hair, lest it gets in your face.'

■

The two of them sat on the beach for a while before getting up and going for a walk. It was a pleasant day, there were a few people on the beach, holiday-makers and parents with toddlers who were running around, playing with toy shovels and kicking up some sand. After a long walk on the shore watching the rustling waves and swooping seagulls, Malika got back to her spot, under a tree and stripped down to her swimsuit. Adi was smitten by what he saw. She began rubbing sun tan oil on her legs and arms and asked him sweetly, 'Will you do my back?'

'Sure,' he said, taking the bottle of lotion from her hand. She could feel his breath on her back and they were only a few inches away from each other. She moved back a little more, drawing closer towards him as he rubbed suntan all over her bare back.

'Nice tattoos, what does this one mean?' he asked, touching her upper back. She had two tattoos, one Latin inscription on her upper back, just below the nape of her neck. Another design was on her lower back, one she was a little embarrassed about. It was something she had got done in Goa, egged on by her then husband, while she was drunk and understood little of what was going on.

'It's in Latin, it means "come in peace",' she said, turning around and gazing deep into his intense eyes.

'Oh, that's interesting,' he said. She leaned in, drawing her lips closer towards his, when they heard a shout, and Aditya turned his gaze in the direction of a volleyball that was rolling towards them.

'Oye, could you please pass us the volleyball,' someone shouted. Aditya got up to throw it back to the college group. The moment passed. They both moved to lie down and read for a while, she noticed Aditya looking distant and confused again, almost grimacing at his novel. He sat up and stared far out into the distance at the setting sun. The deep blue sky was now illuminated with an orange glow, and the seagulls were fast disappearing from the horizon.

She moved closer and requested him to pose for a picture that she clicked on her iPhone. She posted the same on her twitter account with a message that said, 'A fine catch at the Zandvoort Beach near Haarlem'.

'What are you doing?' he asked with interest, turning his gaze away from a flock of pelicans to her.

'Tweeting,' she said.

'You're into that, huh?' he asked, taking her phone to read her tweet; the next second he was smiling, while she nodded her head, turned on her iPod and lay back down.

'What are you listening to?' he asked with some interest, as she turned down the volume on her iPod.

'John Lennon…' she said perkily.

'Not bad, I thought it might be the Spice Girls or Pussycat Dolls,' he snickered.

'Yeah right, why the fuck would I listen to them? I'm not thirteen,' she said turning her nose up at him while he laughed before taking out an earplug from her ear and putting it in his.

'Adi?' she said sitting up for a moment, turning off the music and closing her book.

'Yes, Malika,' he said turning his gaze to meet hers.

'What if Ruheen didn't exist? What if you were flying out to Amsterdam on work, and imagine if I was someone you met in Amsterdam. *Kaho na*, what would you say to that?' she asked, looking at him searchingly. Aditya turned his gaze from her to look at the calm sea and turned it back on her again.

'I'll say I would be a very lucky guy if that was the case. You're smart and rather attractive; charming and graceful…you're a very interesting woman.'

'Am I?' she asked with a mock grin, while he began to look away.

'But that's a hypothetical situation,' he said. 'And then, there's how I feel about Ruheen.'

'What if I was this single guy with no Ruheen in the picture but you were flying out on work while still in a relationship with your Sandeep?' he asked, putting her on the spot.

She gave him a friendly push, 'He isn't my Sandeep anyway! He's a damn wanker I was mistakenly in love with.'

He looked at her with a raised eyebrow. 'Okay, it would be

tough, you would have to work for my affection, but it wouldn't be impossible,' she said pushing her hair behind her ears.

'*Aah,* right! So you'll have it easy, while I'll have to battle the impossible! Nice, very convenient, bloody hell!' he said with a grin, taking a sip of water from his flask.

'What's a conquest without a battle?' she preened.

'Do you want to head back, my lovely conquest? What would you like to do tonight once we get back?' *Ruheen is probably sipping tea, watching the sunset or she might be out for a drive with Varun.*

'Let's let our hair down and party. I haven't partied in a long time, it'll be fun,' she said with repressed glee.

'Sure let's do that. Your bathing suit and your tattoos are quite a hit with those college boys. A couple of them have been trying to get your attention for a while.'

'I know, I did notice them, they're cute.' She blew them a kiss and waved goodbye much to Adi's astonishment, as they stood up to get dressed and leave.

■

They managed to get back to her hotel a few minutes past 9 p.m. Aditya decided to go and get dressed at his hotel nearby and come back for her in an hour. Soon, he was back wearing a smart dinner jacket, a new pair of grey Levi's and blue shirt and nice shoes. He had styled his hair to give it a spike at the front, and he looked very impressive for a troubled lover.

'You look adorable,' he said as he saw her walk towards him in her designer pale blue dress which showed off her legs and revealed much of her back till her hips.

'Thanks, let's go. Where are you taking me?'

'I was thinking of Flexbar—they redesigned the place around the time Ruheen and I came back for a holiday. It's quite happening.'

There we go again, she told herself.

After hailing a cab, they got to the club at 11 p.m. and decided to skip dinner, thus heading straight to the bar. After a few rounds of martinis they hit the dance floor. The bar was set up with two spaces, one playing electro and other playing hip hop. They moved from one space to another, and back again. Both of them had a few more drinks along the way, and danced their hearts out for the next few hours, with little inhibition. She was surprised to see that Aditya was good with his feet, didn't show off like her ex did, held his own and matched his step with hers. The couple had eyes only for each other and were oblivious to the other couples of mixed orientation who surrounded them on the dance floor.

After matching steps to Kanye West's latest hip hop anthem, they decided to leave at 3.30; people were still walking into the club as they walked out. They managed to get back to her hotel in a few minutes and Malika staggered out of the cab.

'Why don't you come up for a bit, Adi? You can take another cab back to your hotel; it isn't far, is it?'

'Okay, I will. No it isn't, it's just a couple of blocks away. I can walk it from here actually.'

'That's good then,' she said tugging on his arm as he settled the fare.

They took the elevator upstairs, Aditya looked away from her on the way up; and on getting off at her floor he followed her into her room. There was a lot of sexual tension in the air between them. They looked like two people who wanted each other, but had held back. It had been this way since the afternoon at the beach.

Malika pulled Adi by his collar towards her, and kissed him softly on his lips. He hesitated for a moment and then kissed her back. He ran his hand around her mostly bare back and kissing her softly and sensually on her lips and neck, while she swooned, whispering his name and telling him to take her.

He opened his eyes to look beyond her, outside the window, seeing couples walk together with their arms around each other, and he heard the sound of church bells ringing. It took him back to a moment, a moment spent with Ruheen in better times.

'Ruheen!' he said suddenly, almost startled by what they were getting up to. 'I can't do this, I love Ruheen,' he said, sitting down on her bed with his hand on his forehead.

'It's been close to six months—she's been in Shimla all this while, bonding with her childhood buddy, as you've mentioned. She hasn't bothered to check how you're doing, and you're sitting here and ruining your life over her!'

'I'm sorry, Malika, but I love her. I need to try and make things work, I've made mistakes too,' he said with some hesitance.

'Yes, I know how much you love her and the whole deal. It's time to get over it, and move on with your life,' she said, raising her voice.

'How can you say that? I've known you for a few months; she's been the love of my life for years.'

'Can't you see that she's with someone else? She seems content with that Varun chap, spending all her time with him. She needs someone else, Adi, someone who can give her that attention and help her deal with her insecurities. She's probably found that person, and you're not that guy. In your life from what you've told me, work came first, and then there was Ruheen. Both of you had a chance to make your relationship work, but it didn't happen for whatever reason. You have to let her be, I don't think she's going to come and don't think you guys are meant for each other. There I've said it.' She looked irate, and didn't want to hold back any more.

'I can't believe you're saying that. My being here, doing this job, putting myself through all this, is about her. We're still together, who says we can't have another chance? I know I made mistakes, and things didn't quite work between us. But I'm about to change that—in a way, I already have,' he said firmly, before walking out of her room and shutting the door behind him.

She struggled to sleep, with thoughts of him and memories of the last couple of days together. She felt like an idiot as she had begun to fall in love with him.

■

The next morning, Malika did an early check out, and leaving her bags at the hotel, she took a boat ride on the canal, exploring the city before she left for the airport.

She wished Aditya would come back and try and make amends for what happened last night. She felt cross with him for walking out on her like that.

Aditya woke up late with a splitting headache. He felt a mix of anger and confusion when he thought of what nearly happened last night. He found it difficult to shake Malika out of his head, telling himself that it was not real and that she was just a young infatuated girl, given the little time they had spent together. But memories of the moments they spent over the past couple of days, a few months ago in Paris and now in Amsterdam shook his belief that with Ruheen it was true love...was she in fact something in the past he was yet to let go? He wondered why this had happened to him just when he and Ruheen were trying to make sense of where their relationship stood. *Why am I being tested like this? Here I am trying to work things out with Ruheen and another girl is drawn towards me. To make it worse, she's a friend and a colleague.*

Malika, he believed, was chirpy and free-spirited; her beauty was less obvious than Ruheen's, but it was, in fact, infectious in a way; it kind of grew on him after he spent some time talking and getting to know her. She came across as someone who was clear-sighted and fun to hang out with, which was a rare combination.

He got to the airport late, doing an online check in. He didn't want to bump into Malika. He wanted to call her and check if she had made it to the airport in time, but he decided against it. He found it strange and it felt weird, as he began to feel sorry about letting her go away like this. He had half wanted to go down to her hotel and be polite. He wanted to take her out for breakfast, and take her on the boat ride on the canal, as promised. But he couldn't get himself to call her at her hotel or go down and see her before she left.

He wanted to put some distance between them. The more he thought about it the more he felt guilty about last night. He felt like he had cheated on Ruheen, though nothing really happened.

She had clearly wanted more than friendship with him, and this was certainly more than what he could offer under the circumstances. He didn't want to make it any worse for her. He realized that it's hard enough falling in love with someone who does not reciprocate your feelings.

He knew what had to be done, as he walked towards the departure gate for his flight to Munich.

2 weeks later...

'Good morning,' Ruheen said, walking into the living room looking sleepy.

'You've only half-woken up, and you still manage to look stunningly beautiful,' Varun said with a broad smile.

'Shut up! You can't digest your breakfast without first flirting with me,' she said, with her trademark pout.

'I believe you like honesty,' he said, turning his attention back to the sports page of the newspaper.

'Varun, did you read this?' Ruheen shrieked. She had just finished her cup of coffee with jam and toast, and was getting up to check on Nana, when she noticed the headlines in the newspaper next to her.

Former minister's son kills himself in Chail

Former Minister, Yashwant Chaturvedi's son, Vishal Chaturvedi, twenty-eight, reportedly shot himself at a cottage owned by his family, near the sleepy little hill station of Chail. The Shimla police broke into the cottage after the caretaker informed them that Vishal had not left the cottage in two days and was not responding to his calls or pleas to open the door. Sub Inspector A.B. Tiwari broke in to find a decomposing body slouched over the dining table. It appears that Vishal had shot imself two days ago, after he sent the caretaker away and asked him not to come back for a couple of days. He reportedly returned from Shimla, bringing home bottles of alcohol, based on the statement given by the caretaker. The police recovered a loaded .45 Remington lying on the floor next to the body, and suspect that Vishal had put a bullet to his head after getting drunk. They have recovered three empty bottles of rum, a bottle of whisky, a half-finished bottle of imported gin and a single half-empty glass. Neighbours claim that Vishal lived alone and didn't have any friends. He would sporadically disappear for days on end and come back after drunken binges in nearby towns. Reports also say that he was unstable, and had been sent away to live in Chail by Yashwant Chaturvedi, who had a strained relationship with his son given his frequent run-ins with the law.

Vishal had earlier been arrested and let off for charges ranging from stalking a girl in college, to vandalizing a pub and assaulting a prostitute and a policeman. He stayed in Australia for three years before he returned to India, a year ago. Opposition leader Chaturvedi said that he was 'shocked' and 'grieved' by the untimely demise of his only son. The family refused to answer any questions. Forensic reports claim that a single bullet was fired from the gun found next to the body, which caused Vishal's death. The police also confirm that five unused cartridges in the barrel of the gun were recovered.

The police have sent the body for a post-mortem to confirm the cause and time of death. The police suspect that it was a case of suicide, but they are 'investigating the matter'. The state police have swung into action, and have been interrogating neighbours and the staff working for the Chaturvedi family. The police also ruled out robbery, as nothing was missing from the premises. In a recent development, the police also recovered Vishal Chaturvedi's two mobile phones and are examining his call history. They have also confirmed that the .45 Remington assault rifle recovered was licensed to Yashwant Chaturvedi, the deceased's father.

Yashwant Chaturvedi's Aam Dal, are attempting to bury the matter and move on, accepting Vishal's death as an 'unfortunate suicide'. The post-mortem reports are expected to come in by this evening.

Ruheen looked up at Varun, with a look of surprise. 'I can't believe this! I can't believe that he was close by. I don't understand this, people like him are sick in their head, but they don't end up killing themselves.'

'Well, the good thing is he has met his Maker. Now, you don't have to spend any sleepless nights, thinking about some crazy stalker,' Varun said coldly.

'My God, I shouldn't feel like this, but for some reason I feel relieved. I feel like I can breathe again.' He smiled at her, and nodded his head.

'Did you have anything to do with this, Varun? Because I know you, and I sense you do.'

'The less you know, the better it is for you. Remember that I'm always around if you need anything. He deserved what he got,' Varun said, looking away from Ruheen's piercing gaze, and walking out of the room.

■

Meanwhile

Aditya, in a pinstripe dark blue suit, walked out of the tube station at Paddington, and walked across the street to an old pub, named Jimmy Blues. It was past 8 p.m., and the sky wore a dark purple blue shade, while peak hour commuters, ranging from middle-aged executives to young women in business suits and high heels, rushed across the street, towards the underground station. He took a table in a corner, behind a jukebox, and ordered a Corona beer.

Fifteen minutes later, Rohan, in a Liverpool jersey and a pair of grey jeans, walked in and spotted him easily. Aditya came across as being overdressed and a little too polished to be slumming around in a watering hole like Jimmy Blues, which was popular with the working class crowd. After a couple of minutes of polite conversation, they decided to get to the point.

'So what do you actually want? I really want Ruheen's divorce to be over and done with. This is why I've flown to London,' Aditya said.

'Impressive! It can be, if we can come to an agreement...'

'Smells like Teen Spirit' by Nirvana blared over the speakers.

'What type of agreement? Honestly what do you want? You're ill and you have only a few months to live.' Aditya said tersely, with a hint of irritation in his voice.

'That is why I called you two weeks ago. I think my sister was a bit too pessimistic about my condition. See, I was ill, mate, I'm completely fine now,' he said, taking out a report from an NHS Trust folder and pushing it across the table to Aditya.

'That's good for you. Ruheen's lawyers have filed for a divorce in India, why are you refusing to give her one?'

'Isn't so easy to walk away, is it? Not after we've flown her into UK and I've clothed her and fed her for a year. We have a marriage registered in the UK, yeah? She has a British passport, too. It has to be done here. Ask your attorney to file for a divorce here, I'm happy to fight this out...'

'Why won't you let her go? I mean after all you've put her through...'

'I will, at a price, yeah. You see, mate, I've cleaned up my act. No more drinking and brawling for me. I work as a steward at Phil's Steakhouse, round the corner. A fair compensation for her freedom is not too much to ask for, is it?' he said, before he finished his drink and ordered one more.

'You must be joking...'

'I think you are, mate. I'm afraid your girlfriend has got herself into quite a quandary. You see I've done some research. A married woman runs away to Amsterdam, meets her ex-boyfriend there. Then she goes and lives with him in Mumbai, and attempts to conceive a child. I'm happy to drag her out here and have her explain things to the judge, yeah,' he said, calling for another beer.

'How much are we talking about here?'

'I'm looking to move to Sri Lanka and start a little café on the beach. A new life, if you will. Say a 100,000 pounds—I believe it's a fair estimate. I get a new start, you get a beautiful bride.

Now I'm being nice here, she's such a beauty...' Rohan spoke with a devious smile.

'That's ridiculous, are you out of your mind?

'No, mate, I'm not. I stay with my girlfriend now, I need the cash, and I'll be happy to squeal to the police on how she flew out of London on fake documents.'

'40,000 pounds. This, I believe, is a reasonable compensation for your efforts.'

'I don't think so, mate. I'm happy to have her and yourself down here, to explain how a woman married to me was living with you and was about to conceive your baby. I'm happy to trash things out, yeah? I'm not sure you want to put your Ruheen through a courtroom ordeal for the next six months, do ya?'

'No, she won't be put through any of that,' Aditya said, sounding enraged. '50,000 pounds, is as far as I can go...'

'60,000 pounds, and I will sing and dance at your wedding. I'll give her away if you want me to,' Rohan said with a gleam in his eyes before lighting up a cigarette.

'Fine, when can you sign the papers?' Aditya asked.

'It will be done as soon as you wire the money to my bank account in Panama. Ask your lawyer to stay in touch with me. By the way, Tiffany's down the road is having a sale...you might want to buy her a nice solitaire,' he said, standing up to leave. 'Also give her my love, yeah?' he added before walking away from there with a broad smile on his face.

Aditya called Mohan on his way out from the pub as he strode across to the tube station. 'Mohan, there is something important. The property we picked up together in Parel, I want to cash out,' he said.

'Why do this now ? What happened? You know the market is down by 10-20 per cent. Wait for six months,' Mohan added wisely.

'No, man, I need to sell out. This is related to Ruheen's divorce, I want to get her out of the whole thing, before we begin afresh.'

'Adi, are you sure man? These are your savings for the past six years! I could raise money to buy your share out. It's a great commercial spot and it will give us good yields.'

'Mohan, I'm sure, can you please expedite this. I want to finish this whole thing in the next four to five weeks. I'll see you back in Mumbai,' he said before hanging up.

28

A month later...

Ruheen woke up one morning to find that her Nana had passed away in his sleep. His condition had been getting worse for the past couple of weeks, and two days before his demise, he could just about open his eyes and call out Ruheen or Varun's name. Aditya, meanwhile, was in Amsterdam on a business trip to finalize the launch of a spate of new products.

'Ruheen, hi, it's me. I'm afraid there is no flight that I can get on to for the next thirty-six hours! I've even considered going to London and flying out from there, but there's an eight-hour stopover. I wouldn't get there till tomorrow night...'

'You're not going to make it in time,' she sobbed at the other end.

'I'm very sorry, you stay strong all right? I'll try to come as soon as I can...' he said. He could hear her crying softly on the phone.

'Adi, it's okay. At least it's all over for Nana! You don't have to come here, Adi. I'll see you in Mumbai in a week,' she said, biting her lip and holding back her tears.

'Okay, I'm sorry again. I should have been there,' he said before she hung up on him.

He tried to make it back to the funeral but he found it impossible to work it out. A number of international connections had been cancelled or had been delayed due to the fog in Delhi. The weeks following his return from Shimla were busier than the weeks preceding his short trip.

He was sucked into dealing with a different crisis every day; he had people leaving, people in different divisions not getting along and more. Aditya was under fire from the Board for getting rid of Fresh, and increasing the marketing spend on Enigma. His division was still in the red, and he had assured them of a turnaround by the next quarter as Enigma was getting stronger and they had a number of new products in the pipeline.

Aditya felt guilty about not being able to make it, not being by Ruheen's side while she went through losing her only family. He tried calling her three times a day for the next few days. Most times, she didn't take his call. She did a few times, and didn't really want to talk to him. She was busy going through the motions of traditional rituals that had to be performed.

Ruheen and he spoke very little during the next three days; they exchanged messages on and off, he believed that she was under severe strain due to her Nana's demise after his prolonged illness; she didn't have much to say when they did speak. She had begun to grow colder and distant towards him over the weeks preceding her Nana's death.

▪

Four days later…
'I've arranged to have Priya dropped off at the Chandigarh Airport tomorrow. Let me know if you need anything else,' Varun asked a sullen-faced Ruheen. Both of them had stayed by her Nana's side for the last few days, days when he struggled to open his eyes and say their names.

'Thanks Varun,' she said sipping on her hot chocolate with tears in her eyes.

'You're planning to go back to Mumbai?'

'Yes,' she said with some hesitation. She played with the chain around her neck.

'When do you leave?' he asked reluctantly.

'In a couple of days, maybe,' she said, gazing at the star-lit sky.

'I'll see you at breakfast then,' he said, before giving her a hug and kissing her on her forehead. He had left work aside and stayed through the ordeal with her. He hadn't gone back to his room or the hotel.

'Varun, wait! Stay, we need to talk,' she said. He sat down next to her on the couch; she moved closer to where he sat, and rested her head on his shoulder, before she broke down.

29

Three days later…

Ruheen returned home a week after her Nana passed away. Aditya got an SMS saying, 'I've just landed, could you please come home early?' He managed to take the rest of the day off, and went home immediately.

He walked in to see her sitting at the table with her hand on her chin and a cup of coffee before her. She wore a black and grey cashmere sweater and a pair of old jeans. He noticed that she looked pale and stressed out, with dark circles under her eyes. He had decided on asking her to marry him, and thought about the solitaire in the pocket of his blazer, the one which Nikhat and Aparna, Anuj's wife had helped him pick up.

Aditya walked up to her, and kissed her on her forehead. 'I'm so sorry about Nanaji, baby,' he said.

She had her hair let loose about her shoulders and he ran his fingers through her tresses, stroking her hair gently. She looked up at him with a lost, faraway look.

'Sit down, Adi,' she said with firmness in her voice. He took a seat opposite her. Aditya figured that they would talk things out for a while before he apologized for not being able to make it for the funeral. He planned to take her for dinner to Olive, where he planned to go down on his knees and propose. He had also planned to leave Indiana Products in six months after launching the products at the end of the quarter and bringing some stability to the bottom line. He had planned to find something that would give him a chance to live and breathe. Her divorce from Rohan had come through two weeks ago, and her now ex-husband was preparing to move to a secluded beach somewhere in Sri Lanka.

Ruheen looked at him with tears welling up in her eyes; he moved his chair next to her, 'Give it time, it will be all right. I know how much he meant to you, but you were with him in his last days. I'm sure that meant the world to him.'

She mustered her inner resolve, and said looked at him with conviction, 'I'm leaving you, Adi. It's over, you and me, we're done. I can't do this any more.' Tears were running down her cheeks, while he sat there stunned, with a look of despair.

'I'm done trying to convince myself. I love you Adi, but I'm not sure if I'm in love with you any more. I don't think I have been, for a few months now. I'm going back to Shimla tonight, and I don't want you to stop me, please!'

'Ruhi, come on! This is outrageous, we love each other. I know you're mad at me but...'

'Adi, I'm leaving you...' she said, biting her lip, while he pushed the chair away and stood up.

'It's Varun, isn't it? You've been having an affair with your childhood friend and neighbour in Shimla? After all we've been through you're leaving me for that guy? You've been having an affair with him, is it? I can't believe you're in love with someone who is a recovering alcoholic living off his family wealth, damn!' Aditya was furious and flung his car keys across the room.

'Adi, stop! You don't know how difficult it has been for me. I've had a difficult life, Adi, please don't do this to me! I've lost the person who raised me; I lost my baby less than a year ago.' She cried hysterically, while he turned his gaze to her bags, she had already packed a couple of additional suitcases. She was leaving him for good.

'What time do you fly out?' Aditya asked, sounding less bitter, but completely shaken by her actions.

'I leave tonight at 8.30 for Delhi. I'm sorry, Adi, I hope some day that you will forgive me, I tried....but you and I, it isn't working any more. It been a while actually, and we've tried too hard…'

'And you've fallen in love with someone else! It's the story of my life. What am I supposed to do, Ruheen? You tell me, what am I supposed to do?' he said frightening her with an insane look in his eyes and shaking her delicate frame with both his arms. He took out the ring he had bought for her, put in on the table, picked up his car keys and walked out of the apartment. He heard her sobs till he banged the door shut and headed down the stairs.

He drove back to his office, and stormed in, alarming a lot of people with his dishevelled look. He sat down at his desk, holding his head. He couldn't think any more, he couldn't speak to anyone, about what just happened. After spending two hours at his desk pondering over his sorry life, Aditya drove back home, maniacally speeding through the traffic. He realised that she didn't deserve the way he had behaved with her, not the way he had been over the past few months. At the end of the day, she was the one he loved. If it ended he didn't want her to remember him by these last few actions. He walked in to see her on the phone, and still looking very upset. She hung up on seeing him walk in. Her gaze met his, and it seemed like she was confused for a moment. It seemed to him like she didn't want to leave. He walked up to her and put his head in her lap. She put her arm around him and they both held each other and cried.

After a couple of hours, he took her out for a late lunch and her favourite gelato. They spoke in monosyllables; mostly he sat and gazed at her intently, while she ate a small portion of what she ordered. They came back, and she spent some time handing over documents that she had taken care of, for him. They sat down at the table and had a cup of coffee together, when he handed her the divorce papers that had come in. 'You are a free woman now,' he said with a sad smile.

She looked more beautiful to him than she had in a long while; he hadn't looked at her as intently as he had today. He realized that she was no longer his. The equation had changed and she had put a barrier between them, an icy demeanour which was cold and formal.

'It's past 6, let's leave. I'll drive you to the airport,' he said, looking at his watch and avoiding her gaze.

'Why are you doing this, Adi? Do you know how hard it has been to come and tell you what I did? You're making it hard for me; you're making me hate myself.'

'It's also devastating to hear what you told me this morning. I was going to ask you to marry me today; I don't believe that's going to happen any more. Driving you to the airport is the least that I could do.'

She looked at him, and looked away. She stood up, and they both took her suitcases down. They drove to the airport in silence. Aditya remembered the day they first came home from Amsterdam, days when she was insecure and frightened at the prospect of living in India. He remembered how she held on to him, and how they made love on his single bed when they had gotten home.

'Take care of yourself, Adi. Good luck with work and everything. I'll always remember the good times we shared. Thanks, for everything you've done. You made me live again, and I did love you with all my heart while it lasted. I want you to know that!' she said with some difficulty, at the airport. 'I'm not sure I feel the same about you any more.'

'I always will love you, Ruhi...'

'Don't say that, Adi! You'll find someone more secure, more deserving of your love. Someone who maybe wants the same things that you do,' she said contemplatively. He realized then that all of the last two years had been about him; about what he wanted to accomplish and how he wanted to live.

'I'm willing to change anything you want, Ruhi. Please give me another chance. Let's try to work this out, don't leave,' he said, looking at her pleadingly while the wind blew in her hair. People standing around were looking at them. It appeared to them like the two were a couple having an argument.

'It's a little too late to make amends, Adi. In the past one year, we've been together but we've actually been miles apart. I'm sorry, take care,' she said embracing him for the last time and kissing him on his forehead.

'I'm still here if you change your mind Ruhi, I love you,' he said with resolve, mustering a faint smile.

She nodded her head; bit her lower lip, while looking at him painfully. Tears began to roll down her cheek; she walked up to him and rested her head on his chest. She walked away pushing her trolley, turning back just once to wave goodbye.

He tried calling her in an inebriated state later that night but her number was no longer reachable. She had cut him out of her life. *I guess it makes it easier for her that way,* he told himself.

■

That night...
Ruheen walked out of the airport, she looked tired and stressed out. She caught Varun's eye, he was waiting for her.

'I'm sorry to make you come all the way,' she said, before giving him a hug.

'It's okay. It went badly in Mumbai, I can figure,' he said, stroking her hair and putting his hand on her head.

'Hmm, it was. I feel so horrible; he looked so dejected and heartbroken,' she said softly with tears in her eyes. 'He was nice to me, despite how it ended. He had a ring and had planned to propose.'

'He's a good guy, I need you to be sure about this situation...' he said, as they walked with her trolley towards his car.

'I am, I'll be okay,' she said, getting in and strapping on her seat belt.

■

A week ago...

Varun tried to pacify an upset Ruheen, she had been crying uncontrollably for the past half-hour. He wondered what he could do to make her feel better.

'I've decided to leave Aditya,' she said, wiping her tears.

'Ruheen, take it easy. You aren't in a frame of mind to take this decision. Take some time off, relax,' he said, stroking her hair.

'No, Varun, I've made up my mind. We're done; I can't see us being together,' she said firmly, before pouring herself a glass of water. Her nose and eyes were red and her cheeks were flushed. He hadn't seen her this upset before.

'I am going to tell Aditya my decision when I go to Mumbai in a few days.'

'What do you plan to do? Are you going to stay here? Stay here, it's a good idea.'

'I need to be away from here, Varun, and you understand the reason why. You're a friend, but I need some space to figure certain things out. I'm not ready to get into anything now, and me being here is only going to lead to us getting together. I'm not sure I want that, at least not yet.'

'Fair enough, you do what makes you happy,' he said sportingly. 'I'm still here.'

'I need your help, Varun.'

'Tell me.'

'I want you to take the Haveli and convert it into this home stay accommodation you spoke about. It is a heritage bungalow with some great views. I'm sure there would be takers.'

'There will be, in fact I'll move up here myself. I'm tired of living in a hotel. Besides the first floor wing hasn't been used for years. It can be restored and I'm sure we can do well...'

'That's nice, and if you can then give me some advance rent

it will help. Like two years' rent in advance or something. Priya runs these restaurants in the food court of a shopping mall in Gurgaon. She is open to me taking up a small counter and starting a small pastry shop. I want to do it, I want to do my own thing,' she said softly. She had mustered up her inner resolve and was determined to change her life. He realized that she had thought this out clearly and that her mind was made up. She had been unhappy for months, and the relationship with Aditya seemed to be crumbling, with both of them barely communicating.

'Okay, good idea, I'm proud of you. Let me see what I can organize quickly,' he said.

'Another thing...' she said, putting her palm on his.

'Say.'

'I need you to be there for me. It may sound selfish, but I need your help and support to do this, it's going to be tough...'

'Don't worry, I'm with you. No matter what your decision is, I'm going to support you. Anything you need,' he said.

PART III

Here and Now
2009

'But who can say what's best? That's why you need to grab whatever chance you have of happiness where you find it, and not worry about other people too much. My experience tells me that we get no more than two or three such chances in a lifetime, and if we let them go, we regret it for the rest of our lives.'

—HARUKI MURAKAMI *(Norwegian Wood)*

30

Three months later

Aditya walked across to Frankie's shack near his apartment in an old kurta and cargo shorts. He had just returned from a tiring day trip to Delhi dealing with the launch of a new Enigma body spray and had a quiet air of despondence about him. He had no time to think, no time to feel lonely or blame himself for everything that happened. There was no time for self-loathing; he was a hired hit man with body sprays, gels and hair oils to sell and fat cat shareholders to keep happy.

He quickly picked up the usual katti roll and was heading back to his apartment, when he was accosted by a stranger.

'Sir, one minute please,' the scruffy man said, taking out his mobile phone. He looked rough and seemed like he was in the wrong neighbourhood. The phone was expensive, and he wore Adidas loafers.

'Yes?' Aditya asked.

'See this, top class models, college girls, very sexy. Tell me what you want, I'll offer good rate. I'll arrange home service,' he said, leaning in closer to Aditya, and tried to show him images on his handset.

'I don't think so...'

'Dekh lo sir, akele ho. There will be no problem, *chinta nahi.* Very good escort service. I can arrange special massage also. I'll give you first time discount.'

'I'm not interested, man,' Aditya said, with some irritation. It led the pimp to back off but not before looking at him with annoyance.

He got across the street and upstairs to his apartment. He poured himself an Absolut Black vodka double shot with soda, and finished the roll quickly. He turned on some music, and sat back with his drink.

'5.15 a.m.' by Mark Knopfler played in the background, as he closed his eyes and sipped on his drink.

The doorbell rang. He went up and opened the door to see Vidya, Mohan and their son, Aarav standing before him.

'Happy birthday, Uncle!' Aarav said gleefully, before stomping in. Vidya and Mohan muttered birthday wishes too, with plastic smiles. They were worried about him.

'Mummy said I can cut the cake along with you. I picked a Ben 10 cake; I know you'll like it.' Aditya nodded along and smiled faintly.

'Why was your phone switched off earlier? I tried again and it only rang. Why can't you pick up your phone? Or call back?' Vidya admonished him.

'I was on the flight to Delhi this morning, and was later passing through security on the way back, sorry.'

'I see you've been eating junk...' Vidya said, noticing the katti roll wrapper on the table.

'Dude, it's your birthday. Can you put on a more cheerful song?' Mohan asked, looking for the remote for the music system. He picked up Aditya's glass of vodka and took it to the kitchen, wanting to avoid it drawing Aarav's attention. Aarav was oblivious to the conversation among the adults. He was busy staring at the cake he had chosen. 'Can we please cut it now, Mummy?' he asked pleadingly. His mother ignored him and kept talking to Aditya at the dining table.

'Uncle, where is Aunty Ru?' Aarav was standing next to Aditya with an innocent smile on his face.

Aditya looked at him with a blank expression on his face. Framed pictures of Ruheen were still plastered on the walls. 'I've told you so many times, she's gone to Shimla. Her Nanaji is not well,' Vidya said in stern voice.

'Where is Shimla?'

'Far away in the mountains where it snows,' his mother explained.

'When will she come back, Uncle? She promised to buy me a toy train for my birthday.'

Aditya looked away. 'She'll be back soon.'

'You come here, how many candles do you want?' Mohan asked. Aarav didn't stir, he continued standing there and looking at Aditya.

'Uncle,' he said shaking him, 'Is Aunt Ru dead?' he asked, making a small face.

'No,' his mother said, rather sharply.

'No Mummy, do you know Sanjay? His uncle, died. Everyone told him that his uncle has gone abroad. One day he came to know that he had died.'

'It's nothing like that, I'll get you to speak to her tomorrow.' Aarav, satisfied by the answer, turned his attention to the cake once more. Vidya looked at Aditya tenderly as he stared into the distance. Tears welled up in Aditya's eyes; he went over to the kitchen to bring a matchbox to light the birthday candles.

■

Meanwhile

'What are you watching with so much concentration?' Varun asked, walking into the room in his pair of faded Levi's and a ripped T-shirt.

'How I met your mother,' Ruheen said, without looking up. She looked divine in her peach top, and ripped-at-the-knee pair of jeans.

He noticed the calm expression on her face, a far cry from her state of mind, a few months ago.

'Hey, move over, Sparky, it's time for the grand prix,' Varun said, plonking down on the couch next to her. He put his hand out for the remote.

'No, *nahi na,* I really like this show, Barney is so funny!'

'Come on, sweetheart, you can watch a rerun later. It's the first Singapore night race, and Alonso is on pole with Raikkonen. Massa and Kubica are on the next row. I don't want to miss the start. It's going to be an amazing race, set for an amazing finish. Now move over.'

'Noooo…' she said, making a small face.

'Oh, come on. I'll buy you the DVD set of the entire season; I'll take you out for dinner after the race.'

'You sit and watch this; I'll take you out for dinner after this episode. I may even let you watch glimpses of the race during the ad break…' she said with a chirpy voice.

'Yeah, right!' He tried to snatch the remote control from her. 'Let's see who's stronger!' he challenged as they wrestled for the remote on the couch.

'No, Adi, please!' Ruheen pleaded. Varun sat up immediately, stung by her utterance.

'Varun,' he said. 'Not Adi, it's Varun.'

'I'm sorry,' she said with a sad pout, sitting up and pushing her hair behind her ears. 'I told you I need time, a lot of time, but you said it will be okay. It isn't okay. It isn't easy for me.'

She buried her face in her palms. She looked stressed out and confused. He gazed at her dumbfounded; this had happened the first time. The first time he heard her utter his name in three months.

'It's okay, it's an honest mistake, relax. I know it's going to take a while for you to get used to wrestling with me on the couch. Let's watch this show, shall we? What is it about?'

She looked up at him for a moment, sullen-faced, then broke into a smile. She leaned closer to him, put her head on his shoulder and told him about Barney, Ted and the rest.

Happy birthday, Adi, she thought.

31

A month later...

Aditya looked up from his laptop screen to see Mr Kishore walk through the door. He immediately got up, and walked up to his former boss who looked frail, and like a shadow of his past self.

'I've not been myself lately. Been getting on with age,' he said with moist eyes, and a forced smile. 'I got back three months ago.'

'You don't look so good.'

'Yes, well you always think that you will have time to do what you really want once you retire. You know, do the things you always believed in. But I feel I don't have the energy any more, I'm tired. Anyway, let's not talk about it,' he said firmly, sounding fatigued.

'I'm sorry I haven't seen you in a while. I had no idea that you got back from your son's place in London. I would have come...'

'Relax,' he said leaning back. 'I didn't inform anybody. How are you?'

'I'm fine. Work is going great; we are launching a new...'

'I didn't ask how the work was, did I? I was with Anuj a short while ago. He told me about you and Ruheen. You have separated?' he asked, with a piercing gaze.

'Yes, a couple of months ago. Things didn't quite work out...'

'When I advised you to stay in the job, I didn't mean that you should compromise on your relationship. I'm worried about you, son.'

'I guess it wasn't meant to be,' he said, looking away. 'What do you plan to do?'

'I don't know.'

'But you must! Don't become like me. I worked all my life

in one company. Everything else took a backseat; today I realize what I missed. I didn't see my own kids grow up, though they were before my eyes...' He had a faraway look in his eyes.

'I agree with you, and I plan to quit in a short while. I can't do this any longer; this isn't what I want to do with my life.'

'It's good, that's a wise decision. Come home for breakfast on Sunday, we'll talk. You should come home more often and spend time with me. Chatting with you will help me kill time,' he said with a wry smile, before he heaved himself up from the chair, and headed out.

■

Meanwhile...
Ruheen was busy at the Mall, setting up the display for the pastries of the day. She was busy coordinating with her staff, explaining to them the ingredients in each of the new pastries.

Her phone rang. 'Yes, Mrs Singh, of course I remember you. *Haanji,* it's possible. You want one eight kg chocolate delight for the 20th, right? I'll have it delivered to you. Sure don't worry about the payment, I'll collect it from Tania later,' she said before hanging up.

She was inundated with orders every day. Ruheen's selections were a roaring success in Delhi. From every order she delivered to, she got a few more. She had doubled her staff in three months, and was planning to open another little counter in a Gurgaon based Mall.

Her phone rang again. She smiled.

'Ms Oberoi,' he said at the other end.

'Mr Shetty,' she preened.

'What's up?'

'I'm busy! I have three orders for this week.'

'Hmm...'

'Can I talk to you later tonight?'

'Really?'

'Stop being funny! Don't we talk every night? You don't let me sleep properly…'

'Why talk on the phone when we can meet?'

'What?'

'I can see you standing there, looking absolutely delicious in your black business suit. It's the most delicious thing in your pastry shop actually.'

'Shut up! Where are you?' she said, going red in the face and looking around. He walked up to her.

'I can't believe that you drove down all the way to Delhi,' Ruheen said, looking surprised. 'It isn't safe you know; the roads are bad, with the fog in the morning.'

'I haven't seen you for two weeks now. You didn't come home last week, either,' Varun said, with his arms on his hips. He looked exhausted.

'You know how busy it is. Setting up Selections in the Mall has been quite a challenge. The Mall management have all kinds of rules and compliances…'

'Hmm…its okay, it's worth the sacrifice.'

'Let's go home, it's past 7 already. What do you want to do? You should get some sleep.'

'Let's go out to some nice place.'

Later at her apartment, after Varun had taken a shower, he asked 'And business is good these days?'

'So far, yes,' she said with her hand on her chin, wondering which dress to wear tonight. She took out a snazzy blue dress designed by her friend Sheetal Mirchandani in Mumbai. Varun planned to take her out clubbing. 'It's been picking up as people have gotten to know about us.'

He wrapped his arms around her waist, and kissed her hair, and then her cheek. 'I missed you a lot; the weekends are unbearable without you.'

'Hmm…' She smiled to herself, loving the attention she got

from him.

'It's so hard with you here in Delhi and me in Shimla.'

'It's okay, you're here now. Stay a couple of days longer this time,' she said, putting her arms around his neck, before he leaned in to kiss her.

32

Two months later...

'Adi, do you remember the Shrewsbury biscuits we got at Kayani in Pune? You remember we went there, a few months ago?'

'Yeah, I do,' he said, looking up from his newspaper. He was enjoying a lazy Sunday morning in bed with Ruheen.

'I really want some, Adi! I'm craving for them right now,' she said, making a baby face.

'You mean right now?' She nodded her head, as he sat up.

'Okay, get dressed, let's drive down. It's Sunday anyway, and there shouldn't be much traffic.'

'Are you sure?'

'Yeah, let's go.'

'But you just got back from Chennai last evening. You must be tired.'

'No, I'm okay. Why don't you get ready?'

'I don't know how long you'll put up with me. I'm hungry, tired or irritable all the time.'

'Sometimes it's all the three,' he said with a laugh.

'Shut up, it's all because of your baby.'

'I'm sorry,' he grinned. 'It's your baby too.'

'Will you continue to love me, Adi?'

'What is this about now?'

'No, I'm worried! I'm getting really big, I have these mood swings...'

'Relax, I love you, and always will. Now let's go and get those biscuits you want,' he said, patting her cheek.

'Let's pick up chocolate mint gelato from downstairs,' she said.

'Since when did you start liking that flavour? You hate it! That's one of my favourite flavours.'

'I'm not surprised, because that's what the baby seems to want.'

'Hey, what are you thinking of, muffin? You seem to be in another world. Your coffee is getting cold. These Shrewsbury biscuits are yummy,' Varun said, as he chomped on yet another one.

'Nothing, yes they are very nice...' she said with a faraway look in her eyes.

'Yup.'

'Varun, when you have kids, what do you have in mind? As in, what would you like them to become?'

'I can't have kids alone, by myself,' he said with a suggestive smile.

'Oh, shut up! Tell me,' she said, leaning in with interest.

'I guess they will be smart, rich and successful. They wouldn't have to go to Berkeley and come back to sell tel—*maalish* for sure. I haven't thought about it so much, but I don't think I'll enjoy having noisy kids running around. I'm going to send them away to boarding school, just like how we both went to such schools.'

'Why boarding school? I went there because I lost my folks. I won't send my kids to boarding school...' she said, sitting back and folding her arms.

'Okay, don't worry, we won't send them. We'll raise them in Oberoi Haveli,' he said, while she gazed at him, looking unconvinced.

'Why do they have to be rich or successful or famous?'

'They don't. It will be good if they are, I wish I was,' he said. 'I probably am now, but after a few knocks in life. I never really figured out what to do with my life. I moved from one thing to another, till I ended up in Shimla running the hotel.'

'You've done pretty well.'

'Maybe, I could have done better doing something else, though I don't know what.'

■

Meanwhile

Aditya was getting frustrated sitting and listening to a bunch of salesmen bang on about their brand proposition. Unwired was the latest telecom service provider to offer GSM services in Mumbai. So far, their launch had been a disaster, being unable to garner subscribers in significant numbers.

'I believe you need to be more creative around pricing your services, orienting them more towards the youth,' Aditya said. He was running a two-day workshop on marketing strategies to turn things around.

'Offering these different options won't help us meet our sales targets next quarter, sir,' one minion said gruffly, while the CEO, a balding, middle-aged executive, sat back and frowned.

'I believe for Unwired, it will take a more long-term approach to building a brand. You need to market to different segments of the market. Each of your target segments is unique; you have to identify niches...'

'No no, we don't want all this, *neeche-ooper.* What is this? We are a mass market brand. Tell us how to market this like Pepsi or chocolates. We want one message everywhere. Either the best network, or best service or best price,' another minion added, to which the other flunkies nodded in approval. This was the moment he was most awake through the day, aside from the time he kept wolfing down chips and samosas.

Aditya controlled himself, and said in a composed voice, 'I'm afraid you have three other players with eighty per cent of the market. They are established in this market on all fronts. You need to crack away slowly, identify needs that haven't...'

'Arrey, don't you have Sameer Khan and Sapna Patel's number?' the CEO asked one minion, ignoring Aditya.

'*Haan* sir, we met them at the launch party, *hai na?*' one minion asked another.

'Get them in for a meeting. Talk to the advertising and media agency; let's get them on hoardings and on TV. Get the director of that new Sameer Khan movie to shoot it. Just like that Enigma campaign that you did. Why can't you do the same thing for us?' he growled, looking at Aditya.

'Research has proved that this won't work. You won't get brand association…'

'Sir, we should also get that Pakistani singer Aseem Latif to do a jingle,' the samosa-swallowing minion said with a portly smile.

'*Sahi hai,* let's go all out. We need to increase subscribers by twenty per cent,' the CEO said.

'Yes, sir,' one minion said.

'*Haan ji,* best strategy sir,' another one grunted.

'*Unwired for everyone,* how does that sound?' the CEO said scanning the room, as ten heads went nodding in deference.

Aditya stood there wondering what he was doing there. *Why am I here? Is this what my life is about? Is this the life I wanted to build with Ruheen? Is doing what I do now going to bring her back?*

■

A week later…

'So how is it going with the consulting assignments?' Mohan asked. They met for a working lunch at a bistro near his office.

'I've finished a few of them; I have a couple more in the pipeline…' Aditya said with a faraway look in his eyes.

'That's good, I'm glad you're settling into this new thing. It's time to find a nice girl and settle down. It's been more than a year since…'

'I'm not taking up any more of them.' Aditya laughed bitterly, 'I don't think you have a clue, man, I'm not just going to get over Ruheen and marry someone else. I've got to be honest with myself and with this other person. Anyway, here's the thing. I sold my sweat equity in Indiana Products. It's quite a sizeable taking. I want you to manage the funds and invest it for me…'

'I can help you but where are you going?' Mohan asked with concern.

'I'm going to be back and forth on a few teaching assignments for a while. I have a number of lectures lined up in business schools in the south. I need to getaway…'

'Adi, you need to snap out of this, man,' Mohan said in a raised voice.

'I know where I stand and I know how I feel. I can't do this anymore, fuck this bullshit! I need to clear my head.'

33

Two months later...

Aditya got back to his serviced apartment after three lectures on branding and retail marketing to the students of Bangalore School of Business. Moments later, while Aditya was reading *War and Peace*, and listening to David Gray on his iPod, his phone rang. It was Abid at the other end.

'Kishore sir is no more,' he said tersely. 'Will you be coming for the funeral? His wife will feel nice. You were his protégé...'

'I'll be on the next flight,' Aditya said in a morose voice, getting up and walking to the balcony with a dejected look on his face. He remembered his last conversation with his former boss and mentor, two weeks ago. He took the evening flight from Bangalore and headed back to Mumbai the same night.

He spent hours at the airport and on the delayed flight, thinking about his life, the things he had done, the mistakes he made. He wondered about Mr Kishore thinking whether his life was a happy one. *Did he go happily or with a sense of regret for lost time and unfulfilled dreams?*

Aditya flipped through pages of *The Storyteller's Tale*, a book picked up at the airport. He went through the book quickly and soon was at the epilogue, when the aircraft began its descent into Mumbai. He read the same lines three or four times—*'At the end of love there is the unloving, when you can engage in the ceaseless hunt for all those things to be taken out, and somehow discarded; when you can fight against the new roads and try, futilely, to return to what you were before.'*

A few minutes before the light landed, he put the book away, and flipped through a magazine in the seat pocket. His attention was drawn to a column by a famous award-winning novelist talking about the other India, the India that was hungry and deprived; a place where there were no designer shoes or private jets. There was poverty, destitution and hunger. 'There are enough people who are happy selling soap, or working in banks or pushing papers. How many of us are doing something more for our people?' the short piece ended, asking a difficult question.

He walked out of the airport and hailed a taxi to take him to Mr Kishore's bungalow in Juhu as a germ of an idea entered his head.

■

Meanwhile

'So how's it going with the hunk?' Priya asked with a grin.

'It's great; we get on so well, he's also my best friend!' Ruheen smiled. 'It's nice to be in a relationship where the focus is on me and I am the centre of attention. Probably it was that way with Aditya for a while but didn't last…'

'Touch wood, but dear, marriage changes everything. Enjoy the ride for now, after a while everything will be about what is practical and rational. It won't be different with Varun. I can speak from experiences in my own life.'

'Hmm…' Ruheen said, before turning her attention to her phone. She had a message that said—'Come home'.

'Surprise trip again! Varun is here,' Ruheen said excitedly. 'I'd better take off.'

Priya nodded her head with a smile. 'Have fun.'

She walked in to see a pathway lit up with aromatic candles leading up to the living room which was dimly lit with candles. Soft instrumental jazz music played in the background. Varun walked towards her and took her in her arms, 'You're looking lovely,' he said before kissing her.

'This is a nice surprise,' she said dreamily. 'Why is the diwan placed in the centre of the room?'

'Go put on your bathrobe, it's time for a massage,' he said with a grin.

'What, now?'

'Yes, my love. After I've picked up half the stock of massage oils from the Body Shop store nearby, that's the next thing I want to do. Come get changed now,' he said, before patting her lower back.

A few minutes later she was on her back, as he gave her a soothing massage, using sensual oils and lotions. 'Oh, Varun,' she squealed.

A short while later, he took her in his arms and carried her to the bathtub, where a bubble bath awaited them, while aromatic candles lit up the room and a bottle of wine with two glasses was neatly kept next to the bathtub.

'Perfect,' she said looking at him with dreamy eyes.

'I love you, Ruheen.'

34

3 months later…

Aditya walked into the mud house, sweating profusely, tired from looking for the old teacher's humble home in the village. He now knew the dusty bylanes of the little village, one which he couldn't point on a map a few months ago. He was in Pocharam, a forgotten village, in Medak district of West Bengal, on a journey to discover his true self and find a purpose in life.

'Come, come Aditya, *subho aprohano.* I hope you had no trouble finding my little home,' the frail old man said. He wore a vest and white pyjamas and sat erect on a rickety old chair.

'Shona, please bring two cups of chai,' he shouted out, before pulling another old chair for Aditya to sit down. After exchanging pleasantries for a few minutes, he leaned forward, and cleared his throat.

'So beta, what is reason for naming the place Sameer Primary School? Was that your father's name?'

Aditya recoiled, like someone touched a raw nerve. He tried not to look uncomfortable. 'Actually, Masterji, it's the name of a child we were supposed to have,' he said with a faraway look in eyes.

'Hmm…what are you doing so far away from your wife?'

'We weren't married, Masterji…Ruheen and I lived together, we were in love, it was a different life back then. Coming home to the scent of her hair, to hear her gentle voice ringing through the walls, her soft laughter…'

'Arrey wah! Let's have another cup of chai'. Tell me more about her. What does she look like?' the old man perked up with a sparkle in his eyes. It seemed like a more important subject than textbooks, plans for a second school and the curriculum—a discussion they were meant to have. This was the reason why Aditya had paid him a visit in the first place.

Aditya removed his wallet and took out a picture, a Polaroid snap of Ruheen and him outside Arc de Triomphe at Champs Élysées in Paris.

'*Wah tum dono sundor lagcha.* She is very beautiful, you are very fortunate! Why are you sitting here with an old man in a village, when you have such a beautiful wife back home?'

'We aren't married, we never were. We not together any more, I haven't seen her for over a year. I messed it up, drove her into the arms of another man. I had little time for her, being too absorbed with work; I was sometimes focused on rising up the ladder and at times surviving. We were meant to get married, we were meant to have a baby. But life had other plans.'

'You young people today! Where is she now?'

'I'm not sure. Shimla, I guess.'

'You haven't tried to make amends; tried contacting her?'

'No I didn't, not really. I wrote to her a couple of times, the letters were returned unopened,' Aditya spoke pensively.

'When did she leave you?'

'Close to eighteen months ago.'

'And you still love her?'

'Yes, very much so! And I always will.'

'How does she feel?'

'I don't know. The last time we spoke, when we split up, she said she wasn't sure.'

'Does she love this other fellow?'

'I'm not sure.'

'So how do you plan to know sitting here in some hamlet in Bengal? Sometimes people take decisions in anger. She probably is less angry with you now. She probably doesn't realize the depth of your feelings for her. *Arrey* Devdas, go apologize to her. Ask her for another chance; tell her to take you back. Fight for your love. What's the worst that can happen? It's better to do that than to sit here and build a second school in this village, we don't need another one...'

'Hmmm...'

'What? Has all what you've done here like a man possessed been able to get her out of your head? Have you put whatever you're trying to sweat and burn out behind you?'

'I don't want to intrude in her life. She is possibly married now; I want to bring her no trouble. She's had enough trouble in her life already. She's been through an abusive marriage, a guy stalking her. I don't know...'

'*Babu,* enough of this I don't know, I'm not sure, maybe or maybe not. Make sure, it's better than doing nothing.'

'I'll think about it.'

'Do something about it. Naming a school after a child you lost isn't going to change your life or hers. *Chalo,* have another cup of chai before you leave.'

He walked out of the teacher's house and walked towards his guesthouse. The air was warm, and the humidity was high. He wiped the sweat off his brow with a tissue. Walking down the dusty street, he remembered his trip to Shimla a year ago. He had decided to go and talk to Ruheen. He was in a different state of mind then, still living in his apartment in Mumbai, haunted by memories of her.

He remembered having got into Shimla, where he checked into a hotel on Mall Road. He got out of his hotel to eat something, when he saw Ruheen and Varun walking out of Shyam Lal's together, with shopping bags in hand. She wore a cream woollen sweater and had a stole around her neck. Her hair was longer, and had been let loose about her shoulders, she seemed leaner. She had a smile on her face, and laughed animatedly, while Varun said something that cracked her up. Both of them hadn't seen him, or didn't recognize him, with his hair long and his beard. He hadn't seen her smile like that in a very long time. He stayed for a couple of nights in Shimla and decided to go back. He didn't end up meeting her.

Walking into his room at the guesthouse, he thought about what the old Masterji had said, and wondered, '*What if I give it one last shot?*'

■

Two weeks later...
Aditya sat back in his easy chair contemplating what to do next. Since he got back from Pocharam, he realized that he had precious little to do. He had no school to build, no teachers to find. He felt fidgety and irritable. He knew what he was supposed to do but was he going too far was the question. He opened the drawer and pulled out a folder containing two letters that were returned unopened.

He opened them and began reading them one by one.

14 August 2008

Dear Ruheen,
I thought I would write a few lines to you before going for a walk along on the promenade. I had one of my happiest days at work today. I miss you terribly, it's bloody awful without you; I regret not having you around to share my happiness. I finally quit my job this morning! Yes, I did resign like I said I would many months ago. I've decided to start doing the freelance consulting work we spoke about. I might also be able to get a few teaching engagements at business schools. Everyone wants to hear a successful story, and Enigma sure is a successful one. I couldn't have done what I did with Enigma without your love and support. I've realized that the only way I

can be happy is with you. Like I told Nanaji a year ago, 'You're the best thing that happened to my life'. I realize how much I miss you after we've separated—why did we have to go separate ways? Why can't we work things out, Ruhi? We can make things right again, I haven't stopped loving you.

I came back at 6 p.m. to an empty apartment, and watched television for a couple of hours; it's something I haven't done in a long while. I would much rather have sat down and had a cup of chai with you or taken you for gelato, or we could have gone out to celebrate at Hard Rock Café. It makes me miserable to think of the things we could have done or the things we used to do. I miss the smile on your face, and the laughter in your eyes.

Sorry, if you find that this letter sucks! I'm not used to writing letters, at least not handwritten letters to the woman I love. I know that the experience of writing office memos doesn't really come in handy here.

Yours,
Adi

PS—I've learnt to use the washing machine.

∎

8 November 2008

Dear Ruheen,
As you can imagine, I'm missing you to bits. I'm sitting in a hotel room in Bangalore, watching it thunder and pour like there's no tomorrow. The traffic is a mess and the streets are being washed clean. I got drenched by just getting out of the taxi and running into the hotel. I can

see a number of poor people taking shelter under the trees and the ramshackle bus stand across the street. Predictably, they are not allowed to enter the premises of the hotel and take shelter here. Sometimes we think of the misery in our lives, and wonder why we go through the things we do. But I realize now that there are so many people worse off than us. Why are so many of us oblivious to the poverty and sadness around us?

I'm in Bangalore to give a lecture on Market Launch Strategies at a couple of leading business schools. It is better than advising companies on their branding and marketing. All of those I've done freelance work for want me to wave a magic wand and pull out a rabbit from a hat. They don't understand the kind of effort it took to make Enigma a big success. What we learnt through that is something that you can't grasp looking at some slides by a consultant. Each product or service needs efforts unique to the market you're playing in and your own internal environment. You can't do an 'Enigma' with everything. Some of their products are rubbish, many lack leadership and most offer run-of-the mill services which are nothing to speak about really. Let me not get started on this.

I can imagine how this conversation would go if you were here. You would listen patiently for two minutes and then say—'Adi, okay stop now, I don't give a fuck about all this marketing *gyan* really!' I would sulk for a while and we would make up with a kiss. We would then argue about which version of 'Blackbirds' is better. I would say,

'I prefer The Beatles version', while you would say that 'I think the Sarah McLachlan version is more soulful, Adi', and I would agree, wanting to please you because I love you. I love to see you smile when you feel you're right and I accept defeat (not because I agree with you really). I still believe the John Denver version of 'Leaving on a Jet Plane' is better than the Bjork version. Ruheen, I miss every little thing about you.

I wish you were with me right now. Maybe we could have snuggled in bed, had a warm cup of coffee, fought over the remote control and made love. I can't stop thinking about you, Ruheen. I can't stop dreaming of a future with you. I'm surrounded by memories of your soft laughter, the mischief in your eyes, the smell of your hair and the touch of your skin. Honestly, that's what helps me get by.

I hope these dark clouds clear, and there is sunshine again. It's been dark and gloomy since I last saw you.

Yours,

Adi

PS—I make better coffee than you now. This is what Vidya said, when Mohan and she came by last weekend.

Moments later, he picked up the phone and dialled a number. A number he hadn't dialled in over a year.

'Hi, yes this is the Oberoi residence... whom would you like to talk to?' an unfamiliar voice asked.

'Ruheen Oberoi, please,' Aditya said. He felt extremely nervous as this was the first time he had called the residence in Shimla. He wanted to check if Ruheen had received the tickets to Amsterdam and the note he sent with it.

'Sir, she is in Delhi on work at the moment. Mr Varun Shetty is here, do you want to talk to him instead?'

'Yes, please put me on,' Aditya said, feeling enraged.

'Hi, who is this?' Varun asked.

'Shetty, this is Aditya. I sent Ruheen a card with a message yesterday. I was wondering if she got it.'

'Oh Aditya, how have you been, man?' Varun asked and added in a friendly voice, 'I don't know, she's in Delhi at the moment.

She should come here this weekend. I'll make sure she does get it.'

'Can you? You have no issues doing that?' Aditya asked curtly, surprised by Varun's friendly demeanour.

'Absolutely not, man, I'll make sure she gets it. No big deal,' Varun said before hanging up. He wondered what the package was about. He felt it was yet another letter; he would as always, let Ruheen decide what to do with it.

35

Three days later…

'You're finally up,' Varun said, walking into the room and embracing Ruheen. 'Many happy returns of the day, gorgeous!'

Ruheen dreamily took the gift-wrapped box from his hand. 'What is it?' she asked with curiosity.

'Open it later,' he said putting his arm around her.

'Thanks for the dahlias and passion flowers. My room looks really lit up, with these lovely flowers everywhere. Which one is this?' she said, pointing to a bunch of flowers in a basket.

'Blue Bell Tunicate, kind of rare. Just like you.' She smiled appreciatively, and blushed.

'So what do you want to do?'

'Let's have lunch together, and drive down to Kasauli? I have the keys to a friend's cottage. We can spend a relaxed evening there. It has great views; we could do a bit of a barbeque in the evening.'

'Sounds nice…'

'Hey, before I forget, here. This came from Aditya. He wanted me to make sure I give it to you.' He put an envelope on her lap and the look on her face changed to a more serious one.

'Why are you doing this?' she said, sounding hurt.

'I promised him that I would give it to you. Open it later and see what it is. You owe him that much,' he said turning his gaze to meet hers.

'What do you want me do?' she said, looking worried and pale.

'You know best,' he said bracing a smile. 'I'm just stepping down to the hotel for a bit; call me when you're ready, okay?' She nodded, with her mind elsewhere before he walked out of the room.

He walked out of the Haveli with a sense of purpose. He had planned on proposing tonight, after a candlelight dinner in the lawn, at his friend's cottage. *I hope everything goes* according *to plan,* he told himself, before he took out the ring Priya had helped him pick out, and looked at it for 100th time.

Meanwhile, Ruheen opened her drawer and took out the last letter she had received from Aditya, the first one she had accepted in over a year, only because it came from some never-heard-of place in West Bengal.

19 March 2009

Dear Ruheen,

For the past three months I've been in Pocharam district in West Bengal—it's a little hamlet near the border of Bangladesh. It took a couple of days to get here. I took a flight to Kolkata, took a train from there to a little town and then got here by jeep. This place is in Medak district, people call it a Naxalite area and say it is dangerous. Sure there's no McDonald's or Café Coffee Day, they don't have movie premieres here, nor is this a destination for another 'India Fashion Week' event, but it's really good to be in. I've met some of the nicest people in this little village. Their problem is that they are desperately poor, worse off than most people in the poorest countries in Africa. There are no roads, toilets, schools or clinics for the people here. I had first come here during my management internship at SK Products to see a village haat and experience the rural market first-hand, over six years ago. I decided there is no point complaining and bitching about what people have and don't, and what the government does and doesn't do. It's up to us to make a difference and I decided to give it a shot. If Greg Mortenson could do it in Afghanistan, then I realized, so can I. You must read *Three Cups of Tea;* it's your kind of book really.

Given that I don't give a damn about consulting assignments for morons any more, and colleges are shut for their summer break, I decided to come down here and spend some time. I've been put up in a guesthouse which is owned by an NGO that runs medical camps here from time to time. I decided to put in some money and using their resources, we've built a small school here. We've just finished the construction and painting of two classrooms. Tomorrow we begin classes for the children of this village. I've offered to provide breakfast and lunch to the kids who come to school; I hear this is the only way they'll come. Isn't that sad? I loved going to school to run around and play with my friends during lunch and the games session. Here they are sent to help their parents in the fields.

The NGO has agreed to provide them with uniforms and the local government is providing us with textbooks! Can you imagine that? I didn't, when I first came here. But they believe that we have good intentions and that we're doing a good job and want to support us.

Some of the so-called Naxalites built this school brick by brick for minimum wage. We are calling it—'Sameer Primary School'. It's the name you had decided on in case we had a boy. I honestly couldn't think of any other name or probably I didn't like any other name. I remember how you always wished for a boy. I wish things hadn't turned out the way they did. Our little Sameer would be three now if he were alive. I wish...

Anyway, I've set up a Trust Fund in Kolkata with a recurring income which should meet the costs of running this place for years to come. The NGO through their network is helping us find teachers, till then I will teach them some mathematics and English. Thanks to the reach of Doordarshan in these villages, these kids do understand a little bit of Hindi. I hope I can do a good job and make a difference.

I walk through the fields at sunrise and sunset every day; it's truly peaceful out here. The fields are beautiful, rustic and natural. I can hear the birds chirping, and I enjoy plucking mangoes from a tree nearby. Being here has helped me put things in perspective. It was good to get out of Mumbai as I was getting more miserable by the day. I was haunted by images of you all the time. I would imagine you lying in bed with me, I would imagine you bringing popcorn for me while watching a DVD and I would imagine you sitting next to me at the dining table while I ran my toe up your legs. It's strange to have such visions, I know. Maybe I was going crazy; maybe the apartment was filled with memories of our moments of happiness.

Some time back I was listening to 'With or Without You' by U2 and 'Love will keep us alive' by Eagles, our songs! I remember how we used to put the music on and mouth the lines together while lying on the couch. I remember you saying—'Adi shut up! You're spoiling it.' You would then kiss me and make up for chiding me. I wish we could relive those days...

Do you contemplate on giving us another chance, Ruhi? Think about it, there were times when we were great together. We were happy and we loved each other, neither of us can deny that. The only thing missing in my life today is you. I've changed everything that caused problems between us. I don't have that job or the stress that comes with it; I have more time that could help

us build a better future. All you have to do is come
back home.

Yours,

Adi

PS—Last evening I saw the eyes of a tiger during my walk.
Yes, there are tigers in these parts. I just stood there and kept my
mouth shut, thinking about you all the time. Had he attacked
me, I wanted to leave this world with memories of you...of us.
I guess he was more scared than I was; he wasn't around when I
opened my eyes.

She put down his letter, and buried her head in her pillow.
She wondered why he couldn't let go. Why couldn't she let go,
and move on? She picked up her phone and tried Aditya's number,
it went to voicemail.

'Adi, this is me. Call me back when you get a chance,' she
said before hanging up.

A while later, Varun and she were having dinner together.
'What are your plans next month?'

'Why?' She seemed preoccupied and tense.

'I'm wondering if you can take off for a couple of weeks.'

'Hmm...'

'I'm going to book two tickets to Istanbul for us. It will be
nice to get away, what do you think?'

'Okay, that's a nice idea. Should I get you more of the soufflé?
I have some in the refrigerator.'

'Sure, thanks. It's great; it's one of your new recipes, is it?'

'Yes, it is, I'll be back in a minute.' The phone rang at the
same time. 'Why don't you get that?' she said.

'It's Aditya on the line,' he said, walking into the kitchen
and handing her the cordless handset. They looked at each other
with a confused expression on their faces. She reluctantly took the
handset from him, and averted her gaze from his.

'This might take a while,' she said, handing him a bowl of his favourite soufflé, and walked out, towards her room with the handset.

'It's so good to hear your voice, happy birthday, Ruhi,' Aditya said at the other end. 'I hope you got the tickets…'

'I did, why are you doing this Adi? What is this about? Why now? I'm with Varun now, we're in a relationship.'

'I love you, Ruheen, even though we've been miles apart, I haven't stopped loving you. I want us to get married, I want to have babies with you and grow old with you. I want another chance…'

She shut the door to her bedroom and sat down on the bed with an expression of worry and confusion on her face, as she listened to Aditya at the other end.

Varun paced up and down the corridor with an anxious look on his face. *Why now? Why at this moment?* He took out the solitaire he had purchased, and stared long and hard at it.

Thirty minutes later, he knocked on her door nervously.

'Come in, Varun,' she said.

36

Two weeks later...

Ruheen was supervising her staff in the bakery, when she realized that she was irritable. She had been in a pensive mood since her return from Kasauli. She wondered why Aditya did what he did. *Why did he have to go over the top and book tickets to Amsterdam? This abrupt step to reconcile matters, now, over a year after they broke up.*

She felt annoyed with him for messing with her head. She and Varun had been drawing close, and they had started to build a relationship that was working so far. Only six months ago, she had reluctantly begun to date him. This too, taking things nice and slow, and managing a long-distance relationship where either of them travelled to where the other was, on alternate weekends.

She liked what she had done with her life. She had started from scratch and set up the bakery, which was doing remarkably well. She had Varun who doted on her, made her feel special. She had space where she could be herself, and feel good. And then there was Aditya, who still loved her deeply. Aditya, whom she couldn't stop thinking about, despite being away from him for close to eighteen months.

Her phone rang just then, it was a number she didn't recognize. 'Hi, yes, this is Ruheen,' she said, wondering who it was. 'Damn, Shilpa, it's you. Yes, I can meet you anywhere, you're leaving tomorrow? I'll be there in an hour,' she said before hanging up.

She got into her Honda City and sped away from the Mall. Kanye West's 'Heartless played' in the background. She was at Café Turtle in M Block market in an hour. Shilpa, her former sister-in-law, was waiting for her.

'Hey, look at you, you've grown big,' Ruheen said excitedly.

'Yes, three months more. I shouldn't be travelling after I get back. I came here to showcase a short film I made at the World Cinema Festival,' Shilpa said.

'Wow, I'm proud of you. Super!'

'Yeah well, enough about me. Look at you, a smart, successful businesswoman. I love that black dress and those pumps. It'll be a while till I can fit into that.'

'I'm sure you will soon. How's James? He must be excited.'

'Yeah, he has a hard time with my moods. When are you planning a trip to Amsterdam? What's happening with you? Fill me in.'

'Strange that you ask, I'm not so sure about coming to Amsterdam any time soon. Things are pretty good, a little strange. Varun and I have been seeing each other. It's not so bad so far, not sure where it's headed with him in Shimla and me here. But then there's Aditya, who wants another chance...'

'Hmm, interesting! Lucky girl, you,' Shilpa said, looking upbeat as they ordered coffee. 'Ruheen Oberoi, still gorgeous and breaking hearts, I like. I'm quite fond of Aditya; your Varun seems like a nice sort too.'

'I would trade places with you. I feel stressed, but I guess I'll be okay. I like where I am right now, I'm not sure I want to change a thing.'

They caught up on other things, Shilpa's pregnancy, her married life, Ruheen's business and Shilpa's film-making.

'How is my ex-husband?' Ruheen asked, sipping her latte. She had heard that he had recovered. The music at the café got peppier, in keeping with the young clientele who kept pouring in after a day at work. Alicia Keys and Jay Z's Empire State of Mind resonated with the free-flowing conversation and easygoing banter that dominated the space around them.

'He's running a tea shop, somewhere off the coast of Sri

Lanka. He's a completely changed person; you wouldn't believe how different he is now. He calls every now and then to check how I am.' Ruheen gazed at her with raised eyebrows and smiled. 'I guess it's all thanks to what Aditya did.'

Shilpa noticed the change in her countenance. Ruheen shifted in her chair, looking surprised. 'What did he do?'

'I didn't mean to break it to you like this, I thought you always knew. But I think you should know, given your situation. Your divorce proceedings were heading towards an ugly court battle. One which would have had you pulled back to London to answer some tough questions, especially given the circumstances in which you left. It was thought then, that the court would divide your assets, which included your grandpa's estate bequeathed to you, between you and Rohan. Aditya didn't want this to happen. He stepped in, and paid Rohan something like 60,000 pounds to sign the divorce papers and walk away quietly.' Shilpa looked at Ruheen squarely in the eyes.

'What!'

'Yeah, I don't support what Rohan did. It isn't right to make use of a situation. But yes, I hear Aditya did that because he didn't want this whole thing to bother you in any way. You just lost your baby a few months before, and your grandpa was critical. Apparently, he didn't want the situation of an ugly divorce coming up, and upsetting you.'

'But Shilpa, that money must've been his life savings! Why didn't he talk to me about it?'

'I'm not sure, but Rohan jokingly told me that he saw Aditya walk towards Tiffany's on his advice, after paying him off, to buy a wedding ring. But then all of this is in the past.'

Ruheen remained silent and looked shocked. The music changed to a more sombre tune, switching to 'Jessi' by Joshva Kadison.

'Let's go, will you please drop me off at my uncle's at Vasant

Kunj?' Shilpa said, getting up slowly, while Ruheen settled the bill.

'Sure, let's go. You please climb down the stairs carefully,' she said.

She called Vidya after dropping Shilpa off at her uncle's. After much persuasion, Vidya confirmed that Aditya had indeed sold his share in the property he jointly owned with Mohan. She had been sworn to secrecy and Ruheen was supposed to know nothing about it.

She got home, and after changing into her pair of shorts and a sweatshirt, she crawled into bed. She couldn't sleep, thinking about what Aditya had done. She walked across to her drawer and pulled out the tickets and the note that Aditya had written to her.

The note said, 'Please consider giving us another chance, Ruheen. We both had dreams of a life together. We can make this work, we can start again. Because love is all that counts, and I still love you. I can't stop loving you.'

She read it again, and stared at a reflection of herself in the mirror. She put the note and ticket back in the drawer, and got into bed. She read a goodnight message Varun had sent her an hour ago, before she closed her eyes. Her phone rang.

'Are you up?'

'I was just falling asleep.'

'Okay, how was the day?'

'Not too bad...yours?'

'Okay...listen, I'm getting into Delhi tomorrow.'

'Why are you coming, Varun? You just went back this weekend.'

'I need to discuss something with you. It's something important, it can't wait.'

37

On the flight to Amsterdam (three weeks later)
4 October 2009

'Aditya,' she said, turning to him once they had strapped on their seat belts and waited for the connecting flight from Brussels to Amsterdam to take off, 'Why did Ruheen and you separate?' She wanted him to talk about the one topic he had avoided through their conversation from Mumbai to Brussels. Realizing that he owed her that much, he decided to tell her what happened, the way it did, over a year ago. The aircraft began to taxi on the runway; they had a flying time of fifty-five minutes. He turned towards her and began.

'So she is in Amsterdam? Does she know that you're flying out all the way to meet her?'

'No, she isn't in Amsterdam. But she does know that I'm going to Amsterdam. I've sent her a letter with a ticket for her. I've asked her to come down as well. So we could meet at Dam Square, like many years ago, and hopefully, work things out.'

'So you sent her tickets to get there, and you're flying in yourself! For someone in love, you're certainly doing a lot to show your feelings for her. I mean flying out all the way, having her fly out all the way. Do you think she'll come?'

'I hope she will...' he said softly, and withdrew into a long silence. He spent some time going through his diary and reflecting on his memories of moments gone by, while she looked at pictures of him and Ruheen in Amsterdam. Everything in the pictures was the way Adi had described it. Ruheen was stunningly beautiful; much more that Adi had described her to be. She had sharp features and light brown eyes that radiated warmth, a face that one wouldn't forget easily. She immediately felt sorry for Adi. Growing out of love with someone like her would be difficult for anyone. Meghna wondered if Ruheen would take up his offer and fly all the way to Amsterdam to meet him at Dam Square.

A short while later, he realized that he was out of breath. They were to land in thirty minutes, and Meghna was looking at him wanting him, to go on.

'That's pretty much it; the months that followed were a blur. I hated myself for a few weeks, I spent weeks hating Ruheen, while I pined for her. I would open her wardrobe and stare at the empty space with a few clothes hangers lying around. Initially I sent her ten emails a day, telling her that I missed her. She replied, asking me to stop making her cry every day, and to stop sending her those emails. She said that she was guilty about what happened and that we have to move on. I replied to her, but the email bounced back. She had closed her email account. I absorbed myself with work, attempting to take my mind away from Ruheen. I wanted to be proved right with the decisions I took. Six months later, I left the company in a better shape than it was when I took over. Raman hesitated initially, he tried to convince me to stay but quickly put one of his loyalists in my position. They started redecorating my office for the new boss, even before I left on my last day.'

'You've been through a rough patch, Aditya,' Meghna said looking at him with concern.

'Hmm...I'm going to catch a few winks if you don't mind,' he said.

In the seat pocket before him, she spotted Aditya's dairy. Her curiosity got the better of her, and she ended up opening his diary and looked at the pictures of Ruheen and him in better times. They came across as a beautiful couple, like they were straight out of a Monte Carlo advertisement. In her opinion, they had a sparkling chemistry, and Aditya looked truly happy in those pictures. Anyone who knew him back then would have said that he had lately begun to look like a ghost of his past self. Meghna could overhear Aditya snoring in his seat, while she skimmed through a copy of *Lonely Planet*. She felt sorry for him, knowing that he was deeply in love with a woman whom he was no longer with. *Would she come and meet him in Amsterdam? I'm not sure,* she thought.

The depth of his feelings for Ruheen was obvious to her. She also noticed an envelope tucked in his diary that had fallen through. She picked it up and tucked it back in, noticing that it was dated back to eleven months ago and had a postmark— Returned Unopened. *Why was Aditya so persistent then? But if the letters were returned unopened, would Ruheen care to fly all the way to Amsterdam?*

As she struggled to comprehend all this, somewhere deep down she wished for Ruheen to come to Amsterdam. She wanted him to be happy, she believed that he deserved that much. As the aircraft touched down and taxied to a halt, she wondered how the situation would pan out over the next couple of days.

'We've arrived?' Aditya asked sleepily.

'Yes, we're finally here,' Meghna said.

'It was great meeting you, and spending time. It really helped, given my state of mind.'

'You're a sweet guy, here's my card. Call me if you feel like a chat or want to have a cup of coffee.'

'Thanks, you can take my number,' he said, giving it to her.

'I hope it all works out for you tomorrow,' she said, smiling at him hopefully.

'I hope it does. You have a good trip, and a good life, if by chance we don't see each other again.'

'I have a feeling we will,' she said, before getting out of her seat and walking through the aisle with Aditya not far behind her.

∎

A few hours later...

Ruheen woke up with a smile and lazily got out of the bed. *Today is a big day, and I hope it all goes well.* She got dressed and went down for breakfast with Priya and her husband, Anirudh.

'Thanks for letting us stay with you guys,' she said, while they looked at her with a knowing smile.

'You're positively glowing! Aren't you all excited about today?' Priya gushed while Anirudh flipped through the pages the newspaper.

'I am, though poor Varun is tired, having driven all night from Shimla yesterday.' Varun had come in early in the evening and they had gone out for dinner followed by drinks with a group of friends.

'Is he up yet?' Anirudh asked.

'Not yet, I'll wake him up after breakfast,' Ruheen said. 'We have to leave in an hour actually.'

'So are you ready for this?' Priya asked, looking at her searchingly, trying to read her mind.

'I think so...' she said, before finishing her coffee, and heading up the stairs to wake up Varun. She walked in, thinking about the two men who loved her immensely and who had helped put the pieces back in her life. She stopped and looked at the tickets that Adi had sent, and wondered if she had made the right decision.

Her thoughts were interrupted by Varun who had stirred and opened his eyes to look at her. 'Good morning, beautiful, what time is it?' he asked in a sleepy voice.

'It's time to leave, get up, Varun,' she said stirring him.

'Let me sleep. Give me another fifteen minutes.'

'Five minutes, we really need to leave!'

'Okay ten minutes it is, now let me sleep.'

38

Next day...
Meghna waited for her flight back to Mumbai at Schipol International Terminal, thinking about what might become of Aditya. Seeing him walk out of Arrival Terminal was the last she had seen of him.

She wondered where he was and what he was doing. *In an hour from now, he would be at Dam Square waiting for Ruheen to show up. I wonder if she will.*

'This is an announcement for all passengers on Air France flight AF-342 to Mumbai. We are sorry to inform you that your flight has been delayed by an hour due to the delay in the arrival of the incoming flight due to bad weather in Mumbai which resulted in a delayed take off. Your scheduled departure time now stands at 16.15. Thank you and we apologize for the inconvenience.'

She almost cursed the overhead speakers; this announcement meant that she would reach Mumbai well past 5 a.m. and would have to take a taxi down to Pune. She wouldn't be home till after 8 a.m. the following morning, just in time to get ready and rush back to work. She walked over to the doughnut shop and picked up another cup of coffee, thinking about how strange love is, and what it made people do. She turned on her iPod and began listening to 'It must've been love' by Roxette.

■

Aditya took a seat at the same spot, at Dam Square, to wait for Ruheen. He remembered what she wore the last time they came here, the scent of her hair and the colour of her lips. He felt exhausted and sleepy, having slept very little since landing in Amsterdam yesterday. The previous day he spent a sleepless night, one of the many in the past year, thinking about her. He walked about the streets and alleys by the canal before he went back to his hotel at 5.10 a.m., and fell asleep for a couple of hours.

His mind was filled with thoughts of Ruheen, vivid memories of the good times they had shared in this haunting city. The times they spent walking about aimlessly, cycling by the canal and making love in her little loft. When he pictured her in his head, it was clear to him. It was only Ruheen whom he loved. He smiled to himself thinking about these moments of togetherness, which had long been swept away with the sands of time.

He looked at his watch again. She was to arrive in Amsterdam at 3 p.m. on Air France's flight from Delhi via Mumbai, in case she had boarded the flight. He remembered that Meghna, his companion on the flight was to take the same flight out of Amsterdam.

He spent the earlier part of the day wandering about the old places he had been to with Ruheen, he walked around aimlessly for a while, stopping at Madame Tussauds for a while and then at a bookstore for a little bit. He sat down for the next three hours watching people move around, some walking swiftly to catch a tram or towards the Central Station, many walking towards or from the café or tavern across the street, which was filled with young people. He was absorbed with memories of a beautiful woman who should have arrived in Amsterdam, and began to skim through his diary looking at their pictures together in happier times. He didn't feel happy or excited, if anything, he felt insecure and remorseful. He spent anxious moments wondering where he would go from here, if Ruheen decided not to come. He almost nodded off to sleep a few times, having slept very little for the past four nights.

■

'Got in safely and on time?'

'Yes, a little uneasy with the light getting delayed…'

'Are you there yet? What happened?'

'Hmmm…nothing yet.'

'What do you mean? You're in Amsterdam, right?'

'Yes.'

'Where is he? He's showed up, hasn't he?'

'Yes, he has…I'm outside the café, I can see him,' she said with her voice trailing off.

'What's holding you back then? This was your decision, you've not been able to get him out of your head, that guy is even worse…'

'I'm scared, Varun! Can we start again? Can we take off from where we once started?'

'Go up to him, Ruheen, you're there already. Listen to your heart.'

'What about you? Oh I feel terrible, Varun. I always end up hurting…'

'I'd rather be hurt, than you put yourself and Aditya through any more pain. I'll live, don't worry,' he laughed.

It had started growing dark with the sky turning into a shade of purple; the blue jays and pigeons started flying back in droves towards their nests, and the street lights were turned on. She walked silently towards him, initially with slow steps, and then moved faster as she got closer. She had listened to her heart, this is where she felt loved for the first time, where she loved for the first time, and there still was the opportunity for her to make things right.

It was an hour past the time when Ruheen and he were supposed to meet when he felt a tap on his shoulder.

He turned around with a look of surprise to see her stand before him, in a cream kurta and a pair of grey jeans. She was still drop-dead gorgeous with long curly hair and her luscious lips, and she was still the Ruheen he remembered. He staggered for a moment, words eluded him, he walked up to her and wrapped arms around her. He noticed the glow in her eyes and a big smile on her face.

'You've been sitting here all day?'

'Yes my love, as always,' he smiled.

'As always, you won't change, will you? Here I am now, Adi. Where do we go from here?' she asked after they kissed slowly with longing and passion, with the sound of church bells ringing in the background.

'Alfredo's for pizza sounds about right. I'm starved…'

'Let's go big boy,' she said with a glow on her face and laughter in her eyes.

'I'm guessing a little Indian bakery called Ruheen's in Amsterdam isn't such a bad idea. What do you think?' He had a big smile on his face, he still couldn't believe she was here, he felt her breath on his cheek, and the sweet smell of her hair was intoxicating.

'I still think you're a genius…' she said with an impish grin with her arms around his neck and little to separate them.

■

Earlier in the day…

Ruheen continued to sit there with her palm on Varun's knee. She had tears in her eyes, and gazed at him with affection.

'Will you look after yourself? Promise me that you'll harm no one else, even if they harm you in anyway. You'll let it go…'

'I promise,' he said. 'I'm really happy for Aditya and you, you deserve each other.'

'Thanks for all you've done, Varun. I couldn't have been here without you. You made me believe in myself, something I haven't done in a long while.'

'Thanks, for every moment you've spent with me. Besides, I'm always there, no questions asked.'

'What do you plan to do?'

'The same like every day; manage the hotel and the home stays at the Oberoi Haveli. I don't have to come down to Delhi on weekends, so I will have a bit more time on hand. I intend to visit my mother, and meet the sister I never knew I had. My brother plans to come down and spend a week in Shimla with his family, so I look forward to that. After that, there's the skiing season in Kufri...'

'That's wonderful, you're a busy man. I'm glad you've mended fences with the family, I hope to see you very soon, okay?' she said, standing up to walk towards the Departure Terminal.

'Sure, I look forward to that. You take care gorgeous, remember I'm always an option,' he said with a wink, half-joking.

'Varun, shut up!' she said with tears welling up in her eyes. She embraced him before turning around walking towards Terminal D. Varun walked back to his car with a smile on his face. He had a long drive ahead to Shimla, and a lot of work to get back to. The hotel was being set up to host guests for the wedding of the chief minster's son with a former Miss India. A couple of the functions as well as a number of guests were to stay at his hotel and the Oberoi Haveli.

He realized he had done the right thing by not asking Ruheen to marry him, a month ago. It was possible that she would have agreed then, if he had proposed, but he realized that Aditya still held a place in her heart. He remembered how her face lit up when he came back to take the keys he had forgotten in her room. He saw her sitting there and looking at the ticket to Amsterdam that Aditya had delivered in Shimla with tears in her eyes. She had remained very quiet and confused during their evening in Kasauli, despite his attempts to cheer her up. She had often remembered Aditya, and worried about him. He had realized that after a while her anger had dissipated and she wondered aloud if she had done the right thing by leaving him. He remembered what her Nana had said when he decided to pop the big question; this was when Ruheen first came to see him after her return from Amsterdam. 'Aditya is a wonderful boy! For the first time I'm happy that she didn't marry you. That's the regret I had in my heart for years,' the old man had said. He didn't want Nanaji to have any regrets in his afterlife either. He felt relieved that he was not in the way. *It is fate*, he thought. *They deserve another chance.*

EPILOGUE

4 March 2010
In Shimla
'Hi, I'm here for Aditya and Ruheen's wedding. I understand that there's a room booked in my name, from what Aditya wrote to me,' she said to the receptionist.

'You're Meghna, right?' She turned around to look at a tall, well-built, good-looking stranger, standing before her.

'Yes, I'm Meghna, a friend of Aditya's. You are...'

'Varun Shetty, I run this place, as well as the Oberoi Haveli, a short distance from here. That's where your room is booked. Come, let me drive you up there,' he said with a friendly smile, before picking up her bag. 'I really like your tattoo,' he added.

'Yeah, this is a new one, it's the co-ordinates of where I was born and where I live now,' she said chirpily. She came across as someone who was spunky, independent and easygoing. He hadn't met too many like her, especially not in these parts.

'Isn't that giving too much information away, especially for an attractive woman such as you?' he said.

'Maybe...how do you know Ruheen and Aditya? I know that Ruheen is from here, isn't she?' she asked with a friendly smile. She found him dashing, someone who evoked her curiosity. He was good-looking in an obvious way, and had a mysterious air about him.

'She is. Well, she's my best friend and we go way back. Both Aditya and she are people I've know separately for a while.'

'Are you the one she was dating, while Aditya and she were apart?'

'It wasn't exactly like that. It's a long story,' he said, smiling at her. 'How do you know Adi though? Are you an ex-colleague from Mumbai?'

'Do I look like I work for Indiana Products, dude?' With her three tattoos, a boyish crop and her nose ring she certainly didn't look like a corporate climber.

'Well, it might be a good idea to catch up for dinner, if you don't have plans. *Waise*, Aditya and Ruheen are still in Amsterdam, they are only flying back tonight, just in time for the wedding in a couple of days.'

'Sure, sounds like a plan. Maybe you can show me around...'

'I'll be more than happy to, but tomorrow. I have all the arrangements to sort out. I'm the makeshift wedding planner.'

'I can help, I manage events and people, and you could say I have the skills.'

'That's nice; I could use all the help I get.'

'Anyway, I met Aditya in Amsterdam a few months ago, and we've stayed in touch since. He's a nice guy...'

'Amsterdam. Well a lot of people have fallen in love there lately, haven't they,' he grinned.

'Yes, they have,' she said, walking into the Haveli with her bags.

Not bad, I have interesting company for the wedding weekend, he thought, as he followed her in.

'We are fated to love one another; we hardly exist outside our love, we are just animals without it, with a birth and a death and constant fear between. Our love has lifted us up, out of the dreadfulness of merely living.'

—JOHN UPDIKE

THANK YOU

It's a great feeling to be bringing out my second full novel within a few months from the first. Though this one took a lot less time and attention from me, than the spoilt child, *Love, Life & all that Jazz...*' Nevertheless, I'm convinced that this is a better written book.

I thank the usual suspects, my immediate family—Nanima, Mum, Minaz, my brother—Ali and our extended family of uncles, aunts, cousins, nephews and nieces. My Dad, Dadi and my Nana, the memories and lessons you taught, continue to inspire me to be a better person.

Thanks again to the inner circle—Mayur, Saugata, Sapna, Manoj, Manish, Asher and Samah, Nikhil and Pooja, Vikram and Sheetal, Dave, Naveen, Nibha, Pranav, Seema, Dr Peyvand, Deepa, Evo, Pratibha and Varun. I couldn't have done it without your support the first time, and couldn't have done it again without each of you standing by me.

Thanks in no small measure to Rikin Khamar, fellow author (and sufferer), dear friend and a brother, for everything he encouraged me to do with this book, and for advising me keep it real. He played an important role in the success of *Love, Life & all that Jazz...*' and has done the same for *Another Chance*. Rikin has pushed me to elevate my writing to the next level, and I hope you like the results. Thanks to Sona and Amrit for letting me intrude and take away Rikin's time on my writing.

Thanks to Meherzad, Amrita, Kamakshi, Rishita, Vinita, Prateek, Allwyn, Sajjad and those who liked *Love, Life & all that Jazz...* and have supported it on the web, at our events, and elsewhere. Thanks to Cyrus, Nauheed, Purab, Soniya, Ash, Nikhil Chib and Shweta Keswani for their kind and unrelenting support. Thanks to Bishwanath, Kamini, Karan, Deepak, Bagchi, Omair and Paritosh, good friends and talented writers who keep me honest, and are good examples of who and how writers should be.

Thanks to Shweta, Meghna and Kainaz, dear friends and my first readers of *Another Chance* who spent late nights reading frequently updated revised drafts on a computer screen, for their invaluable feedback. Getting a woman's perspective on this one was critical to getting it right, and I hope I have with this one.

Thanks to the dedicated team at Grey Oak led by Jaya Nair, Ali Fajandar, Anisha and Mrunalini Katiyar, my editor. It makes all the difference when you work with the right mix of people.

I can't say thank you enough to Sunny Sara and the beautiful Bruna Abdullah for bringing Ruheen alive. Thanks to the brilliant Nitin Patel and his crew who shot the cover, Elton Fernandez and Anjali Noranha, the hair stylists and make-up artists at the fun filled *Another Chance* shoot. This wouldn't be possible without Minaxi and her team at Matrix Bay and thanks to Mark's support.

Thanks to John Lennon, U2, Mark Knopfler, David Gray, Eric Clapton, Dave Matthews Band, Dire Straits, Bryan Adams, The Eagles, Johnny Cash and Frank Sinatra for your music. Thanks to F. Scott Fitzgerald, Charles Dickens, Ernest Hemingway, Haruki Murakami, Lloyd James, Truman Capote, Roald Dahl and James Frey, my favourite writers for their works, my sources of inspiration.

Finally, thank you Costa Coffee and Java U, places where much of this book has been written.

Ahmed Faiyaz